PIROTICA

PIROTICA

Athena Michaels

First published in 2016 by Telos Publishing,
5A Church Road, Shortlands, Bromley, Kent
BR2 0HP, United Kingdom.

www.telos.co.uk

1

Albert 'Cradle' Whitson rapped firmly on the cabin door.

While he waited for a response, he quickly checked his appearance. His leather boots were shined and gleaming; his white shirt had seen better days, but the ruffle down the front stood proud; his breeches were neatly tucked into his boots, and his red Captain's coat was in place, brass buttons gleaming dully in the dim light.

His hand fell casually to the large cutlass he wore slung from his belt, balanced on the other side by a leather holster in which a short-barrelled gun was stowed. He hoped he wouldn't have to use either weapon that evening – it was swordplay of a different kind that he had in mind.

He rapped on the door again, using one of the rings that adorned his hand to create a louder sound. Surely she could hear him?

Cradle caught sight of his face reflected in the polished metal of a nearby lamp. His chin was lightly stubbled, and the scar that crossed his left cheek was a faint white line. He rubbed his hand over his chin, and then smoothed his unruly hair slightly. He was okay.

Had no complaints so far. In fact, he considered that no-one would actually dare complain … for he was, in fact, the feared pirate Captain Bloodstock the Third.

Cradle smiled. You had to have a proper pirate name. No-one would take Pirate Albert seriously. It was all part of the game.

A frown ran across his face. What was taking this blasted woman so long?

He raised his hand to rap again on the door, but before his ring could make contact, the door opened with a creak.

On the other side was a vision.

Cradle had long been wary of the other Captains in the area. You had to be if you didn't want to find yourself with your gizzard being sliced out in the middle of the night. Most of them were just like him: grizzled sea dogs, only older and more cunning. But this Captain … well, she was different. And there was the main difference right there. She was a woman. Female captains didn't come along very often, mainly because most women were wenches at heart, wanting only to wash and cook and see to their man. But every so often a woman of rare spirit and character came along. One who would not be broken. Mirabella del Otraxa was such a woman.

When Captain Mirabella opened the cabin door wide, Cradle's eyes swept down her, head to foot.

Her brown hair was long and fell in curls down around her shoulders. Her eyes were brown, smouldering pits, and a slight smile played over her rouge-smeared lips. He could see her white teeth lurking in her mouth.

Her chest was cinched by a blue corset that pushed her breasts up and created a valley of cleavage to which his eyes were constantly drawn.

Her waist was small and held by the corset, and below, her hips flared out, clad in tight velvet breeches that hugged her thighs. Then her legs fell into a pair of high, blue leather boots just above her knees. The boots presented a lovely aspect to the bare floorboards, as her feet were perched on stiletto heels, making her a good five inches taller than she actually was.

Cradle had even seen her fight wearing those heels, and she was an excellent swordswoman indeed.

Mirabella smiled, and enjoyed the man taking her in. As a woman in these difficult times, she had to use everything at her disposal, and a bounteous pair of breasts, slim waist and killer legs had been her saviours when her fighting skills had not.

'Why, Captain Bloodstock …' She smiled again. 'The third.'

Cradle was somewhat flustered, and, rubbing his hand on his breeches, held it out to her.

Mirabella looked at it for a moment and then took it in her own hand.

She is warm, thought Cradle, and his eyes moved away from her cleavage to see her small hand holding his. Her nails were painted a ruby red, and shaped into perfect ovals. All except the nail on her little finger. For some reason that had been shaped into a sharp point.

'Milady,' muttered Cradle. He really needed to get his act together here. He was a feared Pirate Captain, after all.

He cleared his throat, and with some effort, shifted his gaze to Mirabella's face. 'We have matters to discuss.'

Mirabella kept hold of his hand, and gazed steadily into his eyes. 'Indeed we do,' she murmured. 'Indeed we do.'

Cradle blushed, and allowed himself to be led into the cabin.

Mirabella released his hand and gently closed the door behind him.

'Have a seat, Captain,' she said, and gestured to a wooden bench, covered with fine pillows and a velvet throw.

Cradle looked around the cabin. It was just like his. There was a sturdy desk against one wall, covered with parchments and maps. Compasses and quills were littered on it, small pots of coloured inks stood in a rack, and to one side was a sturdy bound book – the Captain's log. On the other side of the cabin was the bunk. This was more lavish and opulent than his own, bigger too. This also was swathed in velvet and pillows of all colours. The comfort of it reminded Cradle that Mirabella was female after all, even though her shape would really never allow him to forget.

On the walls were hung a variety of lamps, some of which were lit, giving a dull glow to the room. Cradle noted a couple of whips hanging to one side, as well as some spiked pikes and other objects that he was sure were used in Mirabella's discipline of her crew. One of the problems with being a female Captain was that the crew tended to underestimate their leader, which meant that she had to be forever on her guard and prepared to dish out punishment to those who dared to defy her. Even if she wanted to show mercy – a trait that, when rarely given, was often appreciated by crew – she could never shy away from being hard-line.

For all this, though, Mirabella's crew was noted for being one of the most loyal and constant of them all. While other Captains suffered mutiny and betrayal on virtually a weekly basis, Mirabella managed to command a ship that was rapidly becoming the most feared of all on the seas.

'Drink?'

Cradle was brought out of his reverie as Mirabella held out a flagon filled with some dark liquid.

He took it carefully, looking into Mirabella's eyes and searching for any sign of betrayal. She smiled.

'It's wine,' she said. 'Just wine.'

Cradle looked at the flagon and sniffed the contents.

'Oh, for goodness sake!'

Mirabella took the cup back from him, raised it to her lips and took a deep swig.

'It's wine. Good wine. See?'

She gave him back the flagon, and picked up one of her own from a nearby table.

'To us, Captain Bloodstock.'

Cradle smiled and raised the flagon.

'To us.'

He cracked the flagon against hers, and the two of them drank, but neither moved their eyes from the other's.

Mirabella smiled, but sighed inwardly. She was going to have to move this along a little.

'Captain,' she said. 'Thank you for attending me.'

Cradle nodded and took another sip of the wine. It was good, just as Mirabella had said.

Mirabella sank onto the bench beside him.

'I called for you …' she began. 'I called for you … because I have a need … and of all the Captains … I like you the best.'

In fact, Mirabella had done her homework. Listening in the bars and taverns at the ports, hearing the men discuss what they had been up to, and, more importantly, finding out what the gossip was about the

Captains and their potency and ability in bed.

As a woman, Mirabella liked to be in control, but she also liked … a certain size … to feel … very satisfied … and it seemed from all the gossip, that Cradle was particularly well endowed, and skilled in what she needed.

Cradle smiled and took a larger gulp of the wine. He likewise had heard stories and rumours of Mirabella and her appetite for men, and was hoping to see if what he had heard was true.

'You are most kind, Milady,' he said. 'I hope that our discussions can prove fruitful.'

Mirabella grinned. 'Oh good,' she said. 'I hate all this messing about, don't you?'

She placed her flagon down on the table and turned to Cradle.

He felt a movement in his breeches as he looked at her.

'I love the feel of a man,' she said, caressing the side of his face.

Cradle reached up and took her hand in his. He held it, rubbing it gently with his thumb for a moment.

'Milady,' he said. 'It is true that sometimes we must make … alliances … in order to protect the seas.'

Mirabella captured his hand in hers and started, very gently, stroking her forefinger up and down his forefinger, looking into his eyes as that slight, teasing smile played across her mouth. She nodded, frowning seriously.

'And … and …' Cradle was starting to find it quite hard to think … indeed, it was getting quite hard.

'"And" what, Captain?' breathed Mirabella, gently scratching her red nail against the palm of Cradle's hand.

Cradle tried to compose himself, but the woman was

so compelling. His mouth opened slightly as she brought his forefinger to her lips. Her pink tongue flicked out and caressed his fingertip, and then his eyes closed involuntarily as his finger disappeared into her mouth. The red lips closing around it, and her hot tongue swirling over his skin. She suckled his finger in a way that implied she knew just how to suck somewhere else too. Cradle held back a groan.

Her eyes opened wide, innocent, asking him: 'What? Is that okay?'

He drew in a shuddering breath. He had to try to retain some sort of composure here. He was a man of great experience, but he was acting like a beginner around her.

His finger emerged from Mirabella's mouth and she smiled at him sweetly.

'Now, my dear Captain Bloodstock, you are going to do exactly as I say.'

Cradle looked at her and nodded.

'Take off your shirt.'

Cradle's hands moved almost automatically to his buttons and started fumbling with them.

'Wait. Swap position with me. I want to watch you.'

Mirabella held out her hand and hauled him to his feet. She sat down on the bench where he had been sitting. Her velvet-clad legs were apart, and the fabric was tight against her body. She grinned and leaned forward, her arms resting on her legs. 'I'm waiting!'

Cradle swallowed and restarted undoing his shirt buttons. One, then the next, then the next. When he reached the bottom, he started to pull his shirt off. He felt his usual confidence returning as he tossed the shirt aside. He knew he looked good; constant sword practice kept him fit, and he never shied away from climbing the mast ropes to look out over the sea from the watchtower.

'Nice,' commented Mirabella as his nipples and lightly-haired chest were revealed. Below, she could see the muscles of his torso, and below that ... the beginnings of a hairline that led further down.

Cradle stood there feeling slightly awkward. He wasn't used to being told what to do. It was usually he who did the ordering about. Despite this, he found he liked being the centre of Mirabella's attention.

He looked at her, one eyebrow raised confidently as he waited for her next instruction. Yes, he could play this game. The man didn't always have to be on top, did he?

Mirabella gestured with one hand that he should remove his breeches.

Cradle raised one leg and pulled off his boot, and then the other.

The wooden floor was slightly chilly against his feet but he ignored it. He'd fucked in less comfortable places, and at least this one had all the luxuries of a captain's cabin.

He slowly undid the fastenings of his breeches, and let them slip to the floor, leaving him standing before Mirabella clad only in his thin undergarment.

His excitement was plain to see, however, and the white silk was tented around his cock. Mirabella licked her lips in anticipation. The rumours about Bloodstock were clearly true, and she could barely contain herself. Her pussy moistened at the thought of riding him, whip in hand. Bloodstock, however, was a tough and feared pirate; how much control would he comfortably give her? With some effort, she pulled her eyes away from his swelling member and forced herself to look into his eyes.

'Come closer.'

He shuffled closer, still playing along, but his eyes

danced over her impressive breasts, as he wondered what they would look like once he untied the corset and freed them. He felt her hands gently touch, and then caress his silk-covered prick, which jerked in response. He closed his eyes. A woman like Mirabella would be a taste of heaven after the usual wenches that played the whore for Bloodstock and his men. She was a rare find. A really unspoilt beauty.

'Goodness me,' said Mirabella. 'What *have* you got hidden in there for me?'

It was a question that needed no answer, and the playful smile in her voice told Cradle that she knew *exactly* what he had for her, and that she intended to make a full voyage of discovery.

Her hand moved again, cupping him and outlining his whole length against the silk material. Mirabella was impressed. Very occasionally she found a man with six inches, and she usually let him live a little longer. Cradle was much bigger than that … impressive. But it wasn't just length, he was thick too, and she had to have him.

She hooked her fingers into his silk undergarment and eased it down over his cock, which sprang out in front of her face, bobbing slightly.

She caressed his balls with one hand, while gently running her fingers experimentally along his shaft. Now free, he looked even bigger. Her cunt juiced at the thought of taking all of him in. Feeling his width stretch her open as his cock pounded into her hard. She pushed the thought away, hoping the reality of the fantasy wouldn't disappoint.

As she continued her examination of his cock, Cradle opened his legs and let her explore the full length and width with her hands. And as Mirabella ran her fingers over and around his member, stroking and touching, rubbing, he hoped that she would soon let her soft pink tongue follow her keen fingers. When she scraped her nails over his inner thighs, that was when his legs trembled. She noticed and stopped moving.

'Why, Captain,' she said, 'you're trembling. Let me help you with that.'

She steadied his cock with her hand, and leaned forward, planting a gentle kiss on the head.

Cradle watched as she parted her red lips and sucked his cock deep into her mouth. She was hot and wet, and he could feel her tongue running over and around his cock head and shaft. God, she was good. She sucked cock better than any woman he'd had before. A lot of them shied away from it, but not Mirabella. As precum seeped into her mouth, she sucked harder, swallowing the juice as though it was the tastiest thing she had ever had in her mouth. Cradle hoped now that it was.

While she sucked and licked his cock and balls, her long nails ran lightly over the tops of his thighs and teased under his ball sack.

He let out a gasp of pleasure.

'My Lady … oh … ohhh …'

'Ahhh,' said Mirabella. 'Not too soon, my darling. I want to enjoy you first.'

She pushed herself up off the bench and held out her hand to Cradle. He took it, and she led him to the bed, turning down a couple of the oil lamps as she went, so that the cabin was bathed in a warm orange glow that flickered over her skin.

She pushed him back onto the bed.

'One moment,' she said, and turned her back on him to rummage through the contents of a small chest she had on one of the tables. Cradle watched her all the while. Her bottom was covered in tight velvet that hugged her as she moved, and her blue boots creaked slightly as she adjusted her footing on the floor. He had never before seen any woman in such total command of her own sexuality. It excited him beyond belief. Far better than the wantons he had fucked, with their eagerly spread legs, and lips that cried out fake love words in the hope of pleasing him. Mirabella, he knew, would never give lip service to anything she didn't genuinely feel. Or was this merely what he wished to believe of her?

She turned back to him, holding something in her hand.

'I'm just going to pop this on you,' she said, smiling. 'Don't worry. It won't hurt.'

She bent over him, and took his engorged cock in her hand again. 'You really are a very lovely, lovely, *large* boy aren't you?'

There was a faint clicking sound, and she released his cock. 'There you go.'

Cradle looked down. Circling the base of his cock, and pressing tightly around his balls was a silver band. It was about a quarter of an inch thick, and held his balls tightly in place. He could feel his blood pumping, and his cock flexed as he experimentally moved his nether muscles.

'It's called a cock ring,' said Mirabella. 'It has an interesting affect on the size down there, and, so I have been told, makes the whole experience just that little bit more enjoyable.' *And longer lasting* she thought. The cock ring compressed the blood around the area, preventing it from leaving the engorged cock, and making the man stay hard for longer. But Cradle would find this out …

Mirabella looked at Cradle lying on her bed. 'Right, then, I guess you'll want me to slip out of these too …?'

Cradle's mouth dropped open as Mirabella's hands moved to the front of her corset. She deftly ran her hands down the catches, opening each in turn, and when she reached the bottom, she removed the corset with a flourish, her breasts falling slightly and then bobbing on her chest under her blouse. They were full and firm. The breasts of a young woman in her prime; and Mirabella was certainly that, despite the appearance of strength and wisdom, coupled with her pirate ferocity.

Next, she undid the buttons on her shirt. Cradle was hypnotised, and his cock throbbed, eager to be in her. He looked down at it, captured by the cock ring, and saw that it was a good inch longer than normal. The head was engorged, and a small bead of moisture had emerged from the tiny smiling orifice in the end and was pearling there.

His eyes shot back to Mirabella as she removed her blouse, letting her impressive breasts free into the air. Her nipples were hard, and Cradle could see her mounds heft and fall as she moved. She seemed to have the knack of making them defy gravity!

Next, she turned her attention to her boots. She smoothed her hands slowly down her stomach, over the velvet leggings, caressing either side of her cleft, and down her thighs to the boots.

She gently tugged one boot off, and then the other. Letting them fall to the floor from her hands with a clatter.

She smiled at Cradle, who was still somewhat mesmerised by her breasts.

'Glad you like them,' she commented.

Her hands moved sensuously to the side of her leggings, and opened a series of hidden buttons there. The tight fabric loosened, and she tugged them down.

She turned her back on Cradle and deliberately bent double as her white ass cheeks were revealed. Her bottom was clad in nothing more, and as she bent to remove the leggings completely, Cradle got a glimpse of her pussy lips, covered with a light downy hair. They were neat and somehow inviting, and Cradle licked his lips.

His cock jerked again, and Cradle realised that the ring was compressing him in a delightful manner. His hand strayed to his member and gently stroked it. He was so, so hard.

'Naughty boy,' said Mirabella, and Cradle's eyes shot back to her.

She was now completely naked before him, standing with one leg straight and the other bent, one hip thrust out and a hand gently resting on her waist.

Her skin was creamy and soft in the dim light. It seemed to glow from within somehow. Her cascading brown hair was shiny, and her eyes gleamed with a hunger that reflected his. She was beautiful, sexy, and Cradle wanted to fuck her until she screamed.

'Let's see how that cock of yours has responded to … oh my.'

She moved to the bed and reached out a hand to gently stroke him. Every nerve in his cock jumped, and he swore his member grew a little more. She ran her nails gently over him, scratching his swollen balls and making him moan out loud.

'I think you like that? Do you like that? Do you like what my little toy has done to you?'

Cradle nodded. 'Yes,' he muttered.

'Yes what?'

Cradle thought for a moment.

'Yes, Captain?'

Mirabella slowly shook her head. 'Not Captain.'

Cradle frowned. What did she want him to say?

Mirabella moved so that she was between his legs on the bed. Her lips moved close to his engorged cock, and she gently blew on him. It was ecstasy.

'Yes what?' she repeated, and then opened her lips and took his cock head into her mouth once more.

If the first time had been amazing, then this was mind-blowing.

Cradle felt the whole of his sensation focus on the tip of his cock. Her teeth gently grazed him, her tongue traced the contours of his cock head, across the tip, spreading his pearl of liquid away, and then down and around the ridge below. She was a demon! 'Yes … yesssss,' he managed to say.

Mirabella removed her mouth from his cock and looked up at him. 'Good. Now. Yes what?'

'Yes … yes …' Cradle wracked what was left of his mind for the right answer. Anything so he could feel her lips on him again.

Mirabella smiled at him and nodded encouragingly. Her mouth seemed to form a word, and as she mouthed it, so Cradle realised what she wanted. He relaxed inwardly, and although this was against all his principles, with this woman he knew he could do it. For the first time in his life, Cradle didn't feel the compulsion to be the one in charge.

'Yes … *mistress?*' he said.

And Mirabella descended on his cock again.

This time she sucked him harder, using her hand again to stroke his shaft, which was noticeably longer than before.

Cradle moaned and writhed under her. He had never felt anything so good.

After a while, Mirabella released his cock with her mouth, and Cradle opened his eyes to look at her. She was feline. Magnificent. And she was looking hungry. Her eyes roamed his face and body, while one hand, he noticed, had crept down to her pussy, and was massaging it gently.

She moved to straddle him, and he helped her get into position over his body. Her skin was warm and smooth, and her hair smelt of some exotic spice. She kissed him gently on the lips, and moved her hand down to his cock. She raised it up into an angle away from his body, and then positioned her own body up over it. She inwardly marvelled again at how big this man was, and how good this was going to feel.

When she was in place, she moved his cock so that the head was lodged just inside her cunt. She then moved her hands to his shoulders to balance herself, and at the same moment, realising what was needed, Cradle moved his hand to his cock to hold it steady.

With a sigh of pleasure. Mirabella sank her pussy down onto Cradle's cock. She was wet and ready, but so tight that he almost gasped in pain as she forced herself down until he was buried to the hilt.

As his cock stretched her open, and plunged all the way in, Mirabella's cunt gushed with excitement. It was so big and so long that it hurt a little to take him, and she believed that she would never get all of him in there. But she was determined to swallow as much of him into her pussy as she could, and as she raised and lowered herself on firm, strong thighs, waves of pleasure poured over her cunt until pain heightened the excitement so much that she could take as much of him as he could give.

Beneath her, Cradle thrust back against her every

plunge and rammed himself deep into her tight hole as hard as he could. With every plunge, his cock ached and throbbed and seemed to grow, but never came, and so his skin became sensitive and the pleasure grew. For Mirabella, the tension inside her grew and grew. It had been some time since she had last let a man into her bed, and she felt those months of chastity now being assuaged. She didn't want to, but started to lose control of her own body.

It seemed like an age, but was only a few seconds, and she was sitting astride Captain Bloodstock, with the biggest cock she had ever seen deeply buried in her pussy.

Thanks to the cock ring, it throbbed inside her, vibrating gently against her pussy walls even as it plunged into her hard and fast.

She took a breath, astonished that she had taken this beast. And then, with no warning at all, she started cumming.

It took her by surprise. She was the strong one. This just didn't happen. But a small vibration turned into a larger one, a tingle deep inside her triggered others, and it rapidly built until she orgasmed over his pulsing cock.

She fell forward onto his chest, gasping as she came hard.

Moaning against his cheek as her pussy pulsed around him. There was nothing she could do. She lay over him, completely weak from the sheer impact of her orgasm. Maybe she really had left it too long of late.

Cradle felt like he had gone to heaven. His hyper-sensitive member had been engulfed by the tightest, wettest, hottest pussy of his life, which had then proceeded to squeeze and massage him as the hot woman lying over him came her brains out.

His hands stroked over her body as she shuddered with aftershocks. After a few moments, she took in a shuddering breath, looked into his eyes and laughed.

'Oh, my goodness. That's never happened before …'

Cradle grinned back. 'My pleasure,' he said.

He gently rocked his hips, causing his cock to thrust a little further into Mirabella, and then to pull back a little.

She gasped again in pleasure, and rocked her own hips too.

After a moment, they were locked in their own world again, as Cradle thrust up into her body, and she rocked and took him in and out.

His hands held her hips as she scooped up her hair and rode him. She was really wet now, and the lubrication made it easier for Cradle to get all the way inside her.

Her breasts bounced, and Cradle took them in his hands, feeling their weight, smoothing the skin with his thumbs, and rubbing them over her engorged nipples.

After a moment, Mirabella realised she was going to cum again. She slowed her movements to savour the moment, and as Cradle thrust into her, she let herself rise and rise and rise until …

'Aaaaaaaahhhhhhhhhhhhh,' she screamed as a second massive orgasm burst through her body. She shuddered and shook as she came, her helpless pussy gushing liquid over the engorged cock that was servicing her so, so well.

She collapsed onto Cradle, burying her face in his neck. Her breathing was heavy, and he stroked her back and sides while she recovered.

Cradle was starting to feel a little discomfort now. His partner had cum twice. Massively. And his cock was starting to feel as though it would burst.

He had come close to cumming with her that time, but as his ardour rose, so the cock ring seemed to press tighter around him, somehow stifling the urge and leaving him unfulfilled.

Mirabella pushed herself up from him, and with shaking legs released his dick from her pussy. She moaned as she felt him leave her body. She felt so empty. She wanted him back in there again as soon as possible.

She moved back down his body and again studied his magnificent cock. The head was purple and engorged, and the veins stood out along the sides.

She took it in her hand and stroked it. Holding it proud from Cradle's body, she gripped it and, using the slickness from her own cum that coated it, gave it a couple of experimental strokes up and down. Her hand glided smoothly along the length, and Cradle gasped in pleasure.

Mirabella grinned. 'Very good. Very, very good.'

She raised her hand to Cradle's face and offered her fingers for him to lick.

'Taste me. Your cock is covered with me.'

Cradle opened his mouth and sucked at her fingers. She tasted musky, sweet and wonderful. He wondered if he might get to taste more of that.

'Now,' Mirabella said, stroking Cradle's face. 'One more thing I need you to do for me.'

She scooted away down the bed and positioned herself on her hands and knees in front of him. He could see her ass cheeks glowing in the light, and her pussy was swollen and puffy from his previous ministrations.

She looked back at him over her shoulder. 'What are you waiting for?'

Cradle hesitated a moment.

'Fuck. Me,' said Mirabella in a whisper, and turned

her head, burying it into a couple of pillows.

Cradle didn't need to be asked twice. He sprung up from his prone position, and, stroking Mirabella's astonishing body once more with his hands, positioned himself behind her.

Mirabella moaned as she felt his cock brush against her sensitive lips, and Cradle used his hand to position himself at her entrance. His cock was so big that he had to arch his back in order to get it there, but once there, he slowly straightened his back, which moved his cock smoothly into Mirabella's ready and waiting pussy.

She cried out at the depth of penetration. This was nothing like she had ever experienced before. This man was magnificent. A true stallion of the first order.

Cradle slowly pistoned himself into her. Getting the feel for her depth and his size. Getting her used to him. Then, once he had the measure, and he could feel her juices starting to oil his cock, he started to move faster. Setting up a regular rhythm of strokes. And now it was his turn to take charge.

Mirabella didn't know what day it was.

Or what time.

Or even what her own name was.

All she knew was the intense pleasure her body was now receiving from this cock that was her world.

She cried out 'Oh … oh … oh …' in time with his fuck strokes.

Cradle smiled; he liked to please a woman.

'Fuck! Fuck! I'm … I'm going to … cum … ag … again!' cried Mirabella. And then she was.

She screamed as yet another orgasm shot through her. It seemed impossible, but it was bigger and better than the others, and Cradle didn't stop fucking her even as she writhed under him. Her arms and legs turned to jelly and her pussy turned to fire. The massive cock kept pounding into her, and she kept cumming and cumming all over it. It hurt, but it was pleasurable – that perfect balance between pain and pleasure.

She gasped and writhed and came and screamed and came and shuddered and moaned and came … over and over and over.

Fireworks exploded in her head, and a blackness rushed to engulf her. She collapsed on the bed, as Cradle slowed his movements inside her.

Cradle was suddenly worried about Captain Mirabella. He had known girls to cry and scream as he serviced them, but never to … to what? She was lying immobile and silent on the bed in front of him.

'Mirabella?' he said tentatively. He stopped pounding his cock into her pussy and pulled out. His dick was dripping with her white juices, stirred up into a froth by his movements.

He touched her ass cheek and shook it gently. 'Mirabella?' he said again a little more loudly.

Fuck! Had he killed her?

That would be a first. He had killed people with many weapons, but never this one.

Cradle was just wondering what to do. Should he get dressed and do a runner, knowing that there was one less pirate ship to worry about out there? Or should he claim the killing and take control of her ship, crew and treasures?

Mirabella groaned and rolled over. A happy smile crossing her face.

'Mirabella!' said Cradle, the relief evident in his voice.

'I told you before,' said Mirabella. 'You naughty boy, you forgot.'

'Sorry … Mistress,' said Cradle hastily.

'That's better,' said Mirabella, smiling. She stretched her body languidly on the bed like a cat. Looking up at Cradle, standing there all concerned, she reached out a hand and took hold of his cock. He gasped. He was still hard as nails down there. No sign of it relaxing, and no sign of him being able to cum himself.

'You are a keeper,' she said in a low voice.

Cradle grinned. At least this meant that he was unlikely to be murdered in his bed anytime soon.

Mirabella stroked her hand up and down his dick again, and Cradle moaned.

'Oh dear … does my poor baby need some release?'

Mirabella teased Cradle's balls with her nails.

Cradle grunted. He really did need to cum. This was starting to feel more like some sort of torture than pleasure. He considered that if he hadn't had this cock ring on, then he would probably have cum much earlier on. Mirabella was so hot and sensual, with a killer body that would cause most men to shoot their load before their cocks ever got near to her body.

There was a gentle click, and Cradle looked down to see that Mirabella had removed the cock ring from him. He felt his balls fall slightly, and the pressure in his cock receded a little.

But now Mirabella had him again. With a wicked grin, she sucked him back into her mouth, and with a skill betraying much practice, suckled and stroked him. Within moments he felt his orgasm coming, and seconds later he was cumming in her mouth. She moaned deep in her throat as he did, and continued to suck and stroke him, draining his engorged balls of every drop of his cum.

Cradle's legs trembled and threatened to drop him to the floor of the cabin, but he steadied himself with one hand.

When he had finished, Mirabella sucked him clean, and then let his rapidly deflating cock plop out of her mouth. She continued to caress him, and looked up into his face. A gentle smile playing over the corners of her mouth.

'Come,' she said, gesturing to the bed once more.

Cradle was hesitant. 'I … I'm not sure I can …'

'Oh, you silly … There will be another time for more of that … I just want to talk.'

Mirabella had a plan. Cradle listened intently as she outlined an operation that should result in pleasure for both of them, while ensuring them notoriety, and wealth to come. It also meant that they would, for the foreseeable future anyway, become partners. So no more looting each other's ships, and no attempted double-crosses or mutinies. The biggest bonus of course was that Cradle would get to fuck Mirabella on a regular basis – something that he was quite keen to do. And Mirabella would get to enjoy the pleasure of being fucked by Cradle on a regular basis – something that she was *very* keen to ensure.

'Let me get this straight,' said Cradle, absently stroking Mirabella's hair. 'You're suggesting that we capture a couple of kids, somewhere in their twenties, and train them to be our perfect sex slaves. To make and mould them into pirates. To make them think like us, but be totally loyal to us. Maybe then to take over the running of each of our ships, so that we can spend more time doing what we want to do?'

'That's about the size of it,' said Mirabella. 'And it's the plan, too.'

Cradle grinned.

'But,' she continued, 'to make it interesting, you will take a female, and I will take a male.'

'That certainly makes it easier,' said Cradle. 'I'm not into men.'

Mirabella nodded. Cradle noticed that she didn't admit to not being into women.

'And,' she said, 'we're to do this through pleasurable coercion, not through pain and torture. Much as I like a little torture from time to time, I feel that it will be easier to break others to our will if they want to be broken … if you understand my meaning?'

Cradle smiled. He really liked the sound of this, especially as Mirabella's hand was gently stroking his balls once more …

2

The sun was blazing when Charlotte stepped from the carriage onto the dockside.

She adjusted her large hat and squinted around.

Behind her, her mother and sister disembarked, her mother's strident tones being heard by everyone within earshot.

'… and the next time I ask you to get us there in time, I don't expect you to take a detour through a field!'

Mother dusted down her dress as though it was filthy from the trip.

The driver nodded subserviently, and headed to the back of the carriage to get the cases.

Around them, there was a bustle of noise, colour and movement. Charlotte loved the docks. She liked the sense of anticipation and of the industrious people who worked there.

She saw a group of tanned and toned boys hefting great barrels, possibly containing rum or whiskey or some such. They made the containers seem weightless as they passed them one to the other in a chain all the way to a large net spread out on the dock. There they stacked them, ready to haul them up onto the waiting ship.

She watched as their muscles glistened in the sun. She realised that her lips had gone quite dry, and so moistened them with her tongue. Something about those boys attracted her.

She shot a side glance at Mother to see if she had noticed, but Mother was, as usual, too busy with herself and her problems even to acknowledge anyone else was present.

'Careful there, easy with my cases.'

The driver was taking the luggage off the carriage and stacking it on the roadside. Mother was fussing around, checking and rechecking that everything was there, and that there was no damage. Charlotte saw her rubbing at an imaginary mark on one of the cases, while continuing to berate the poor driver for his choice of route, the manner of his driving, the colour of the horses ... anything and everything fell short of her exacting standards.

Charlotte sighed and looked away. She hoped that this trip would be pleasant, but was afraid that with Mother there, it would be anything but. Mother had a knack of getting under people's skin, and making them actively hate her within minutes of her starting to talk at them. Because that was what she did. She didn't have conversations – an exchange of information or pleasantries. It was a one-sided diatribe. Mother's way or no way. Painful.

'Which boat do you think we'll be on?'

Charlotte's younger sister Anna came up to her and slid her hand into hers.

Anna was just 16, some four years younger than Charlotte, and because of Mother's overbearing attitude, had so much to learn about the world.

'I don't know,' said Charlotte. 'It might be this one.'

Charlotte indicated with her other hand the large ship they had alighted beside.

Her eyes swept over the wooden sides, studded with windows, and up to the tall masts and rigging that touched the sky above.

All around the ship, preparations were being made. There were sailors tightening ropes, and another party was washing the deck with mops. Yet more were crawling over the rigging and sails like spiders, fixing and checking and ensuring that the boat was truly shipshape.

Down on the dock was a flurry of people. Carriages like theirs were arriving and departing all the time, depositing groups of gentlemen and ladies, who stood on the dock, uncertain until men clutching paper manifests arrived to check with them where they should be and where they should go.

'Look over there!' exclaimed Anna.

Charlotte looked and saw a group of lads dressed in the traditional white and blue, singing as they marched across the dock toward one of the ships moored there.

Anna watched them go. 'I'd like to meet a boy,' she stated. 'I'm sure they must be interesting to talk to.'

Charlotte laughed. 'Oh, you silly thing. I'm sure there will be boys,' she smiled at Anna, 'and I'm sure you will get to talk to some of them.' Charlotte glanced over at Mother, who had finally finished berating the driver and was now looking around like an eagle seeking its next meal. 'As long as Mother doesn't find out,' she finished under her breath.

'Ah! Charlotte. Anna. To me, please.'

When Mother instructed, you didn't hesitate. Not if you wanted to keep things happy, anyway.

The two girls, still holding hands, stepped to where

Mother was standing by the cases.

The driver, realising that there was going to be no tip forthcoming, pulled himself back onto the carriage, and with a cry and a clatter of hooves, drove off down the road.

'What a racket,' Mother said, frowning as she watched him go. 'I'm sure he was after keeping one of our cases. Never trust a man. You mark my words.'

Charlotte and Anna both nodded, realising that this was the only response required.

'Now. Girls. You must stay close to me, and don't wander off. The docks are no place for a lady. Heaven knows what some of these men might get up to. So stay close.'

Charlotte smiled and nodded again, but her gaze drifted off around the docks once more.

As her eyes skimmed over the taverns that lined the road, she saw tables of men, all drinking, chattering and often laughing uproariously at some joke or comment. There were grizzled old sea dogs, white beards down to their chests, nursing tankards of ale, while strapping young lads smacked each other on the back as they too quaffed flagons of amber liquid.

'You stay here. I need to find someone to help us.' Mother would not just wait until someone came to her. No. She needed to be top of the list.

'Yes, Mother,' said Charlotte and Anna simultaneously.

'I don't want anyone stealing our bags while I'm gone.' And with that, Mother stomped off in search of a man with a manifest who could show them where they should go.

Charlotte sighed again. Oh, she so hoped this trip would be fun.

They were heading from England to America, to meet with some nobleman with whom Mother had been corresponding. Charlotte had her suspicions that said nobleman had an eligible son, and that she, or indeed Anna, would soon find that they had a husband … and of course they had no say in this whatsoever.

Charlotte's gaze roamed and settled on yet another group of young men, who were helping to unload another carriage that had pulled up. As she watched, the men gently lifted crates containing what appeared to be chickens down and onto the dockside.

One of the men looked up suddenly, and his eyes met hers.

They held each other's gaze for what seemed to Charlotte to be forever, until she broke it, covering her mouth with her hand and blushing bright scarlet.

Anna didn't notice. She was preoccupied by a queue of people forming by the gangplank up to the ship that Charlotte had indicated earlier.

Charlotte risked another glance at the boy, and he was looking at her again! She quickly looked away. Goodness. What would Mother say!

But here she came now.

'Ah, good. Girls, you're still here.'

What did she think they were going to do! Run off across the crowded dock?

Mother had a suited official in tow. He seemed a little flustered, but then this was the usual reaction from those to whom Mother spoke.

'Now then,' she said in a tone that brooked no dispute. 'I am Lady Cotterington, and these are my daughters, Charlotte and Anna.'

The girls dropped into curtseys as they had been taught, and Mother smiled a tight smile of pleasure.

'We're booked onto the ship *Providence*, bound from England to America.'

The man muttered under his breath, hands shuffling the paperwork. '*Providence* … yes … England … America … Three pm … Yes.'

He looked up at Lady Cotterington, and then at Charlotte and Anna, as though checking that there were just the three of them and that they weren't trying to smuggle others on board with them.

'Yes … Excellent … Follow me …'

The official gestured at the group of lads who had finished unloading the chickens. Charlotte was aware, out of the corner of her eye, that the boy she had locked eyes with was still looking at her.

'You there, lads, this luggage, *Providence*, dock five, follow us.'

The lads moved over and picked up the luggage. Charlotte reached for her own case, only to find that someone had their hand on it already. She touched warm flesh, and looked up into the face of the boy she had seen before. She immediately moved her hand, and blushed once more.

The lad smiled, and hefted her case up without a word. He gestured to her to go first, and the party all followed the official across the dock and toward the line of people being checked onto the boat.

Charlotte looked up at the prow and saw the word *Providence* written there in large, fancy script. This was indeed their ship.

She was aware of the lad standing behind her carrying her case. She could feel his heat through her crinoline skirts, and her legs itched. She was sure his eyes were on her all the time, but when she turned to look oh so casually around, he was instead chatting to one of his friends. Her eyes took in his toned, muscular body, his arms holding her case as though it weighed nothing, and a small anchor-shaped tattoo on his left bicep. There was a sprinkling of sweat across his chest, and she felt a bead of perspiration run down her own neck.

This was certainly going to be an interesting trip!

3

'Room 23,' ordered the First Mate. 'And make it snappy, we leave in an hour!'

James Stoker didn't have to be asked twice. This was his first journey of passage, and he was determined to make a good impression.

He picked up the bedding and headed off to Room 23.

The passageways on the *Providence* were narrow, with just enough room for people to walk down single file, but at the moment, the passengers were still boarding, and so it was relatively easy to get through the ship and to the rooms with the provisions that they needed.

Once in the room, James set about making the bed, smoothing the sheets and blanket, and ensuring that everything was just right. He had to have made at least six beds so far that day, as well as carrying a tray laden with glasses and bottles of wine to Captain Harris's cabin. There was so much to do on the day a ship sailed, and little time to think of anything but what needed to be done next.

James checked his handiwork and smiled. Once you got the hang of it, making beds and folding sheets wasn't so bad.

He left the room and headed out down the corridor once more.

Just before the main stairs, he noticed that one of the cabin doors was ajar, and stepped closer to check on it. Sometimes the cabins were used by stowaways trying to gain free passage, and all the crew were encouraged to keep their eyes and ears open at all times.

He paused by the door, and pushed it further open. A gentle moan came from within.

James frowned, and stood there a moment, listening.

The moaning sound came again, slightly louder this time.

It was a woman.

James was paralysed. He didn't know whether to burst in, or to flee.

The woman moaned again; this time it was a gargled cry of pleasure.

'Oh God, yes Henry, yes!'

As James listened, he heard a rhythmic creaking start up, and each creak was accompanied by the woman's breathy exhalations.

James was in no doubt as to what was happening in the cabin.

The creaking became more pronounced, and the woman began to cry out in time. Moaning 'Yes' under her breath.

James pictured her in his mind's eye. One of the maids, perhaps, or a scullion, and the man … no idea. He didn't know anyone called Henry.

Craning his neck, he spied the woman lying flat on her back on the bed, legs spread, while the gentleman worked at her.

He heard the man moan gently, a soft expression of delight, and the woman cried out louder.

The rhythmic pounding continued, and the woman started to encourage her lover. 'That's it, Henry! Yes! Oh yes!'

There was a sudden increase in the frequency of the creaking sounds, then abruptly they stopped, and the man let out a stifled cry himself.

James imagined that he had just spent himself on the lady, perhaps pulling his cock out just in time to prevent insemination and squirting all over her body.

James grimaced. He recalled several occasions when he had been called to clean up after customers' room parties. Bottles and glasses everywhere, underwear too, often stained and streaked with semen. There was one occasion when a glass was full of the opaque white liquid. Disgusting. The things people got up to!

There was a rustling sound from the room, and James quickly moved away from the door and stepped down the passageway, pretending to check on a deck-plan of the ship that was pinned there.

From the corner of his eye he saw a gentleman emerge from the room, ruddy faced and checking his trouser flies with his hands. It was one of the Mates. James recognised him from the ship's mess.

The man, Henry presumably, saw James and abruptly turned and headed up the stairs to the decks.

After a few moments, the door opened again, and James was astonished to see Molly emerge. Molly was one of the girls who worked in the ship's laundry room, and who often smiled and flirted with him. She was petite and had straight brown hair, which she wore pinned up. Now it was loose around her face, and framed her perfectly.

She was smoothing down her starched uniform, and James noticed that she had her shoes in her hand; her feet were bare and stockingless.

James absorbed himself in the deck-plan, trying to look as though he had lost his bearings.

'Hi, James,' said Molly cheerfully.

James jumped, and turned to look at her. 'Oh … Hello, Molly.'

'You lost?'

James frowned. 'Lost?'

'The map, silly. You're looking at the deck-plan?'

James looked back at the document, and then at Molly again. 'Oh … yes … the deck-plan … yes … I was … I was looking for … Room 40.'

Molly giggled. 'You silly. There is no room 40! This ship has only 35 rooms.' She smiled at him coyly. 'Maybe see you later, James?'

James felt himself blush. Later? What did she mean?

Molly turned on her heel and walked back down the corridor to the stairs, raising each foot to pull her shoes on in turn as she went. At the bottom of the steps, she looked back at James and flashed him a smile. 'See you around, Cabin Boy!'

And then she skipped up the steps and was gone.

James let out a breath.

He liked Molly. She was always nice to him and smiled at him … but now this! She was not the innocent little girl that he had thought, but a woman indulging in trysts with others on the crew. James was no prude, but had decided when he joined the service that he would work hard and ensure he gained a good position. Romantic escapades were farthest from his mind, and although he liked the company of women, he had yet to go any further with anyone.

He ran his finger into his collar and loosened it a little. His cock was stiff in his trousers, a result of his unexpected encounter, and of what the sight of a slightly dishevelled Molly did to him.

How, he wondered, was he going to get through this journey now?

4

The *Providence* set sail at noon precisely.

There was a band playing on the dockside as the ship-hands cast away the thick ropes that tethered the boat to the dock; the long wooden gangplank was hauled onto the boat and stowed; and the engines set up a determined chugging to move the ship away from the dock and out into the water.

On the deck, Charlotte, Anna and Lady Cotterington stood and waved aimlessly at the people watching from land. There was no-one there they knew, so Charlotte had no idea to whom they were actually waving. It was just something that everyone on a boat did when it left.

Down on the dockside she saw the group of lads watching the boat go. The one she had caught the eye of was looking straight at her, and when she gave a shy wave in his direction, he returned it.

Charlotte smiled to herself. Much good it would do. She'd probably be married the next time she set foot on English soil.

She sighed and pushed herself back from the side of the boat, and wandered along the deck, watching all the passengers waving enthusiastically as the ship slowly headed away from the dock, and off into open sea.

The sails creaked as they caught the wind, and all around her were the sounds and smells of the sea. Gulls wheeled overhead, crying in their distinctive voices, and the men who worked on deck called to each other as they prepared the main sails for unfurling, and the ship to head out across the ocean *en route* for America.

Charlotte wondered again what the journey might bring. She wasn't particularly looking forward to meeting some strange man who might have to be her husband. *I wonder if he will even speak English?* she thought to herself.

Suddenly, someone bumped into her, and she returned from her daydream to see one of the cabin crew trying to stabilise a tray with glasses on it. She had walked straight into him!

'Oh my goodness, I'm sorry,' she blurted, and reached out her hands to help.

She steadied the lad, and he breathed heavily. 'That was a close one!'

'I know, I'm so sorry,' said Charlotte again. 'I was in a world of my own.'

'That's okay,' said the lad, smiling at her. 'I often find that watching the land slip away can have that effect.'

Charlotte smiled back. This boy seemed nice. He had a nice smile. She decided to be bold.

'My name is Charlotte,' she said. 'Charlotte Cotterington.'

'Pleased to meet you, miss,' said the boy. 'I'm James Stoker.'

Charlotte curtseyed. 'Pleased to meet you too, Mr Stoker.'

James grinned at the formal address. He wasn't used to the passengers being human in their responses to him

– or even noticing him, for the most part – but it still made him smile when they referred to him so formally.

'I think you can call me James,' he said.

'Well thank you … James,' said Charlotte. 'Maybe we shall meet again on this voyage?'

James nodded. 'It's a small ship, miss. I'm sure we shall meet again.'

'Well then. James. Until next time …'

Charlotte curtseyed again, and continued her walk along the deck. James watched her go. She was dashed pretty, he thought, and friendly too. Maybe this trip was going to be more interesting than he had thought. But still, he wasn't really allowed to fraternise with the passengers, even when they were actually friendly towards him.

Lady Cotterington stopped waving when the people on the dock were little more than ant-size. In her world, she was Queen, and these were her subjects. Of course she would wave to them, just as they would wave back at her! It was the correct and proper thing to do.

Now that they were under way, the next thing to do was to check her cabin, and make sure that everything was suitable. She was sure she would find something wrong – she always did – but then the crew would put it right for her, and all would be well.

'Come, Anna,' she said, and swept off down the deck without even checking to see that her daughter was following.

Anna trotted along after her, holding the hem of her dress up slightly so that it did not foul the floor. She was smiling, and this was all such an adventure for her. She could not remember the last time she had even left the

Cotterington estate – though Mother assured her that they had taken holidays away at some point. It must have been a long time ago.

Across the deck, Lady Cotterington spotted the Captain, and so she headed straight for him, determined to secure her place on the top table for dinner.

Anna saw what she was doing, and sighed to herself. Mother could be very single-minded when she wanted to be.

5

Several weeks later, the *Providence* was nearing the end of its voyage. England was thousands of miles behind them, and the ship was now entering the Caribbean Sea, on its final approach to America. No-one on board noticed the schooner that suddenly appeared on the horizon. It was a small ship, and was overlooked as the crew trimmed the sails and made ready for the last leg of their journey.

On board the schooner, the feared Captain Bloodstock the Third stood on deck, regarding the passenger ship through a telescope.

He smiled, seeing the sails on the ship – still tiny through his spy-glass – billow in the winds.

'One Eye!' he called, and the schooner's navigator hurried over.

'Cap'n?' said One Eye – so called because one of his eyes was covered with a patch. He told anyone who asked that he had lost it in a duel with another pirate, whereas in fact it had been an unfortunate accident with a broom-handle that had caused the injury …

'Steer a course …' Bloodstock checked again through his glass, assessed the course the other ship was taking, sensed the wind speed against his face, and mentally triangulated against the position of his own vessel. '… North West by thirty degrees. Fast as you can.'

'Aye, Cap'n,' confirmed One Eye, and hurried off to the ship's wheel to get the instruction carried out.

Bloodstock smiled again, and looked once more at the vessel that they would soon be approaching. He hoped there would be some good plunder there, and looked forward to working with Captain Mirabella on their little plan.

They had talked, plotted and conferred late into the night, and Mirabella had ridden him to orgasm twice more before he left, giving him ideas and suggestions as to how to coerce and encourage whoever they chose to join them on the seas in a life of piracy and plunder.

He couldn't wait to get started.

On board the *Providence*, all was serene and quiet. The sea was calm, but there was a gentle breeze that kept them moving in the right direction.

James was serving drinks to the passengers, who were variously occupying themselves on the deck. Several older couples were sitting on benches, enjoying the sunshine, while others were standing by the railings, looking out at the empty seas all around them.

From above came the creaking of ropes and timber, as the sails billowed in the slight breeze, carrying the ship toward America. Men worked on the rigging, tightening and adjusting knots, and ensuring that all was well.

James headed back to the mess with a list of more drinks required. This was hard work! He barely had time to think while carrying out his daily duties, and his feet were aching.

In the mess, he saw Molly polishing tables with a cloth. Like many of the crew, she would do whatever was needed, depending on the time of day. Mornings, it was the laundry, washing and scrubbing and drying the sheets and blankets. Then there was making up the rooms, then serving food and keeping the eating areas clean and tidy, and then in the evenings, she would be washing dishes and scrubbing floors … whatever was needed.

James was pleased that he didn't have to do much of the cleaning work. His status on board was lowly, but he was employed mainly to keep the passengers happy, making sure that they had everything they needed.

Molly smiled at James as she walked past him. He had been keeping a keen eye on her throughout the voyage, and on several occasions had listened guiltily outside cabin doors when he had chanced upon her having further assignations with other members of the crew. He wondered if she realised that he had been listening in. It didn't actually bother him if she did, but he was intrigued as to what drew her to characters like Henry. He never seemed to have anyone flirt with him.

His mind flicked to Charlotte and the brief exchanges he had had with her over the past weeks, after their chance encounter on the first day. Maybe he should find out if Lady Cotterington and her daughters needed anything.

James smiled to himself and, retrieving the drinks that had been prepared while he waited, headed off to deliver them.

He was sure he had seen Charlotte down by the stern of the boat, sitting in a chair and reading. He would head down there next and see if she needed anything.

Captain Harris was on the bridge of the *Providence*, keeping an eye on the compass and ensuring that they remained on their intended course. They were, of course, at the whim of the weather; and the wind at present was little more than a gentle breeze. Still, at least the sun was shining and the ship was steady. There was nothing worse than having a full complement of passengers all suffering sea-sickness as the craft rocked and rolled on restless water.

Harris gazed out over the still water, and spotted another craft approaching from the starboard. He narrowed his eyes. 'My glass,' he asked, holding out his hand.

One of the Mates gave the Captain his eyeglass, and he peered through it intently.

'It's a schooner,' he said to himself, studying the approaching ship. As it came even closer, he swept its decks and rigging with his glass. There were men hauling on the ropes and working on deck. All seemed normal.

At that moment, with the ship perhaps 100 yards away, Harris saw a flag unfurl on the main mast. It was a chillingly recognisably sight, but one that he had not previously encountered in his own career: a black background with a white skull and crossbones painted on.

Pirates!

The feared Captain Bloodstock the Third stood on his deck as his ship, the *Nancy*, closed in on the *Providence*.

As the two ships drew nearer, he saw the passengers on the deck of the *Providence* start to take notice. A ripple of alarm ran through them when the Jolly Roger flag was unfurled, sending them hurrying back and forth like startled ants, and Cradle smiled. He supposed that it was lucky for them that on this particular mission he was after some very specific plunder. After he and his crew had seized what they needed, they would leave the others in peace.

The two ships drew alongside each other, and when they were only around 12 feet apart, Cradle gestured to his trained crew to prepare the boarding ropes.

They picked up coils of rope, each with a grappling iron on the end, and prepared to swing them over onto the other ship.

Cradle could now hear the screams and cries of concern coming from the passengers as they saw what the approaching ship intended. The crew of the *Providence* moved among the passengers, trying to calm them, and to get them to return to their cabins.

Cradle saw a man in a white Captain's uniform emerge from below deck. He was carrying a blunderbuss, and was fiddling with the unfamiliar object, trying to get it loaded so that he could defend his ship.

The two ships were mere feet apart now, and at a shouted order from Cradle, fifteen ropes were flung onto the deck of the *Providence*. Fifteen grappling hooks bit into the deck and secured themselves around the railings, and the pirate crew tightened the ropes, bringing the two ships fully together with a gentle bump of hull against hull.

Captain Bloodstock the Third moved forward, and raised his own pistol to point at the Captain of the *Providence*.

'Captain?'

Captain Harris stopped fiddling with the dratted blunderbuss and looked up. Facing him on the other ship was the very image of a pirate captain. Red linen long-tailed jacket, white shirt with a frilled front, leather belts around a pair of black breeches, the legs tucked into a pair of stout brown leather boots.

The pirate captain's face was smiling, white teeth grinning above a neatly trimmed saturnine beard, and blue eyes twinkling below curly black hair, with a tricorn hat atop his head.

What took most of Captain Harris's attention, though, was the pistol in the pirate's hand, pointed directly at him.

Captain Harris swallowed, and let the blunderbuss drop to the deck with a thud.

'That's right, Captain,' said Cradle. 'No need for that. We're just after a couple of hostages, and then we'll leave you in peace.'

'Host ... hostages?' managed Captain Harris, and Cradle nodded.

'Think of this as your donation to the future of pirating,' grinned Cradle.

The pirate turned to his men.

'Slosher, Capri ... off you go ... you know what we're looking for.'

At his word, two of the other pirates leaped across onto the *Providence* and moved among the crew, who just stood there, uncertain what to do.

Captain Harris looked into the eyes of his pirate counterpart, and admitted defeat. He didn't want his ship ending up scuttled and the crew and passengers joining Davy Jones at the bottom of the ocean.

'It's okay, lads,' he called. 'Just let them do what they want to do.'

'Very wise, Captain,' said Cradle, bowing low and flourishing his tricorn in hand in an expansive and affected curtsey.

Captain Harris stood there as the pirates swarmed over onto his ship. How was he going to explain this when they arrived in America!

6

James awoke to darkness.

He could hear his own breathing and his heart beating in his chest, and below that, the faint creak of timbers and the wash of the sea.

He also sensed that he was still on a ship.

And his head hurt.

He groaned and raised his hand to his face. At least he was still alive.

He thought back to what had happened on the *Providence*, and winced. The ship had been invaded by pirates, that much he knew, but rather than just slaughter everyone on board, they had stormed through the cabins, apparently seeking something in particular.

When he was spotted by two pirates, he turned to run, but they were on him like a shot. He was dragged out onto the deck, where a man who was apparently the pirate captain had given him a cursory once-over and then nodded to the underlings who held him.

There was a sharp crack to his head, and he was knocked unconscious.

And now he was in a room somewhere else …

probably on the pirate ship, he guessed. As he lay there, his eyes slowly became accustomed to the dim light.

He moved and sat up gently. Strangely, he seemed to be lying on a soft bed, and the covering was a velvet material.

He looked around, and saw that the cabin was gently lit by an oil lamp hanging in one corner. It wasn't a cell – there were tapestry hangings on the walls, and, as he had noted, the bed was soft and well made.

He tried to stand, and apart from a throbbing in his skull, he seemed okay. He went over to the door and tried it. He expected it to be locked, and it was. He shrugged and turned back to the room.

There was nothing more to do but wait. He sat back down on the bed and put his head in his hands. He hoped that whatever fate the pirates had in store for him, it wouldn't be too long in coming.

Captain Mirabella watched the boy through a gauze-covered part of one of the tapestries. She had decorated the room specifically to hide several peep-holes that she had introduced.

She smiled. Cradle had done well. This was a fine specimen of a man. He seemed young and strong. And not stupid – he had tried the door! She recalled several 'guests' in the past who had just given up all hope the moment they had bee taken, and hadn't even bothered to explore the surroundings they found themselves in.

What she needed now, was to prove to herself that this young man could be moulded into shape … could be trained in a manner that would serve her, and would allow her to control him in return.

She moved away from the peep hole and returned to

her own room, where two of her female crew waited for her.

Both were dressed in simple, loose silk garments as per her instructions, and both had been well trained in the art of seduction. For that was what she intended initially for the boy. To gain his trust, to seduce him, and then to make him hers.

'You understand your instructions?' Mirabella asked the two women.

They nodded. 'The man must be pleasured, and tested,' said the first girl.

Mirabella smiled. 'Good. And then?'

'We shall report back to you,' said the second.

'Excellent. You can start straightaway,' said Mirabella.

She couldn't wait to see how this catch fared.

'No Mama, no, I don't want to,' murmured Charlotte in her sleep, tossing her head from side to side. Then suddenly she was awake.

She opened her eyes and winced. It was bright. Sunlight streamed through a porthole on the other side of the cabin.

But it wasn't her cabin.

She was suddenly wide awake.

She sat up and looked around her.

She was in a fairly bare room. Wooden, as all cabins were, but this was devoid of any trappings of luxury. No silks or pictures adorned the walls. There were no tables or dressers covered with perfumes and unguents, and there were no carpets or rugs underfoot. The bedding she lay in wasn't finely made fabric either.

Just on the other side of the room, there was a low moan, and Charlotte sat still.

Who was that? And moreover, why were she and this unknown person in a room together?

Charlotte tried to think back.

She recalled heading off to bed. Saying goodnight to her mother, and getting into her bunk in the room.

Then she had woken to this.

Strange.

The low moan came again, and Charlotte got out of bed, and padded silently over to a huddled shape under a blanket on a low cot on the other side of the room.

She pulled back the blanket to reveal a girl lying there.

The girl opened her eyes, and started when she saw Charlotte. Then her hand flew to her head, and Charlotte could see there was a nasty bruise growing on her forehead.

'Are you all right?' she asked.

The girl looked at her suspiciously and nodded. Pulling herself into a sitting position on the cot.

'My bloomin' head hurts,' she said. Then she looked around. 'Where are we?

'I was going to ask you the same question.'

The girl studied Charlotte carefully. 'You don't remember, then?' she said.

Charlotte shook her head.

'The pirates?'

Charlotte's hand went to her mouth and her eyes opened wide. She shook her head again.

The girl frowned. 'I was in my bed, tucked up for the night, and then there was a ruckus outside. People shouting, that sort of thing.

'I got up, went to the door and opened it to see what the noise was. That's when I saw them.'

'P – Pirates?' stammered Charlotte.

'Yes. Pirates. There was this burly chap right outside my room. I was face to face with him. And then he clonked me.'

'Clonked you?'

'Yes.' The girl gestured to her bruised forehead. 'Clonked me. See?'

Charlotte nodded.

'And then I woke up here. With you. Who are you?'

Charlotte blushed. 'Oh, I am sorry. Charlotte Cotterington.' She held out her hand. 'Pleased to meet you.'

The other girl sniggered.

'Oh,' said Charlotte. 'Sorry. Force of habit.'

'I'm Molly,' said the girl.

'Molly?'

'Just Molly. Worked on the other ship. Washer, cleaner, housekeeper I was.'

Charlotte nodded. 'I was just a passenger.'

Molly pulled herself to her feet. 'So where are we, then?'

'I have no idea,' said Charlotte.

Molly prowled the room, checking the door – it was locked – and porthole – it didn't open – before returning to the cot.

'Looks like we're in a right pickle,' she said. 'But still. Could be worse.'

'Worse?' said Charlotte. 'How worse?'

Molly looked her in the eye. 'We could be dead.'

There was a click at the door, and James was instantly alert. He did not move, though, keeping his hands to his head as he sat on the bed.

He raised his eyes, and in the dim light, he saw two

women silently enter the room. They locked the door behind them and stood there facing him.

James raised his head and looked at them. First one, and then the other.

They were stunningly beautiful.

The first girl had blonde hair, which cascaded down her neck and back. Her eyes were large, and her face was slim and pretty, with a small mouth, and cute chin.

The other girl was a brunette, and her hair was cropped short, in a style that emphasised her high cheekbones. James could see a tattoo on the side of her neck – a bird of some sort – though in the dim light it was hard to be sure.

Both were wearing silken pyjama-like costumes that clung to their bodies, outlining their firm breasts and narrow waists.

Seeing him looking at them, the girls smiled at James.

'What is it?' he asked, his voice cracking. 'Have you come to kill me now?'

The blonde glanced at her friend. 'No. We're not here to hurt you.' Her voice had a faint lilt to it, which James couldn't place. He was used to hearing English, and French for that matter, and English spoken in a French accent, but this girl's voice was none of those.

'I'm Roxy,' said the brunette.

'And I am Inga,' said the blonde.

And then they both moved to sit next to James on the bed.

James noticed that the brunette, Roxy, had in her hand a goblet. She gave it to him.

'Here. Drink this.'

'What is it?' asked James suspiciously.

'Something to help with the pain,' said Inga. 'We heard you hurt your head?'

James's hand automatically went to the lump on his skull where the pirate had hit him.

He sniffed the goblet, and it smelled of alcohol mixed with a sweet, woody undertone – perhaps one of those fancy spirits that the gentlemen liked to imbibe after dinner.

'Go on,' said Roxy. 'It won't hurt you.'

'Do I have any choice?' asked James.

The two girls smiled in reply, and so James shrugged, and sipped the liquid.

It was strong, and burned as he swallowed. He started coughing.

'Steady there,' said Inga. 'Take it easy.'

'I'm … I'm okay,' James spluttered. He took another sip, and this went down much easier.

The girls smiled at him again.

'What … what do you want?' James asked.

Roxy was already running her hands over James's neck, gently massaging him there.

'We just want to be nice to you,' said Inga. 'There's no law against that, is there?'

James was distracted by Roxy, who was running her fingers through his hair.

Inga got to work gently removing James's formal tie, and started to unbutton his shirt. James wasn't sure what to make of all this. He sipped his drink again, and let Inga take his shirt off.

Meanwhile, Roxy was slowly massaging his neck with her hand. It felt really good.

'Let me help you with these,' said Inga.

She helped James to his feet, and Roxy slid around behind him on the bed. Inga's clever fingers unbuttoned his breeches, and slid them down and off his legs. She gently ran the palms of her hands over the bare skin on his legs, gently kneading with her thumbs. Her head was cocked up, looking at James as she did so.

Roxy then pulled James back onto the bed, cradling him in her arms. Her hands smoothed over his shoulders and down his chest, gently brushing his nipples. James drew in a breath as her thumbs gently circled his nipples, making them stand on end.

James now had an idea where this was all going, and as he had no say in the matter, he decided to play along. Plus, the drink had made him feel decidedly warm and fuzzy – he didn't think it was drugged, just a strong alcohol.

Roxy's hands smoothed down his pectorals and to his stomach, stroking him. James didn't realise that the girl was actually checking how strong and defined his muscles were.

Over his shoulder, and out of sight, Roxy grinned at Inga and nodded. She was very pleased with this young man's body.

'What's your name?' asked Inga, as she stroked her own hands up James's legs and to his bare thighs.

'It's James,' he said, enjoying the feelings of two pairs of female hands stroking his body. He felt himself start to react to this, but again, as there was nothing he could do, he just sighed and went with the flow.

'Well … James,' said Inga, her foreign tongue rolling around his name, 'I think we'd like to have a little fun with you. If that's all right with you?'

James could have laughed, but he didn't. Instead he sipped his drink again, and gestured around the room. 'Well, it looks like I'm not going anywhere else … and I seem to have a little time … so, yes, that's all right with me.'

Inga grinned, and her hands slid up his thighs still

further, her thumbs now stroking up under his undergarment to the crease of his upper legs.

James felt Roxy behind him bend her head and gently kiss the side of his neck. Ripples of pleasure ran up and down his body, and Inga felt his legs erupt in goosebumps.

James sighed.

'Oh, you like that, do you?' teased Roxy, kissing him again.

James would have answered, only Inga was now stroking her hand over the front of his undergarment, feeling the large, hard shape of his cock, which was hidden beneath.

With this sensation, and the feeling of Roxy gently kissing his neck, it was starting to get difficult for James to think, let alone to speak.

He felt cool air on his cock, and realised that Inga had eased the front of his undergarments off. He lifted up his bottom to help her, and felt them slide away.

Cool hands stroked up his legs again, and Roxy nuzzled and nibbled at his neck once more, making his cock leap and bob in front of him.

As Inga's hands reached his balls, and gently caressed them, Roxy's hands stroked around his body, and her fingers found his nipples.

James was in ecstasy.

As one woman kissed and nibbled his neck while her fingers stroked and gently pinched his nipples, the other ran her fingers up and down his erect cock.

Inga dipped her head, and James felt the warmth of her lips on his cock head, her tongue gently caressing him, stroking and rubbing at the point where his foreskin joined his cock.

He gasped as his cock was engulfed in her mouth, red

lips clasping him, and the hot, wet sensation of him being suckled as Inga moved her head up and down on him.

It was all too much. With a groan, James came in her mouth, his cock pumping and jerking as Inga sucked him.

Roxy giggled, and watched over his shoulder as Inga sucked all James's cum from his cock. While she watched, she toyed with James's erect nipples, gently flicking them.

Inga licked his member clean, all the time gently rubbing his balls and shaft, and encouraging every drop into her mouth.

James gasped for breath. 'Oh … oh my … I … I'm sorry,' he said.

Inga let his cock free from her mouth. She smiled at him, and he could see that she had swallowed all of his cum.

'That's okay, honey,' she said.

'Mmmm,' said Roxy by his ear. She gently bit on his earlobe and then kissed it before releasing him.

Inga stood and smiled down at James. 'I think you have lots of potential, master James,' she said.

James looked up at her. 'Potential? Potential for what?'

Inga and Roxy looked at each other and smiled.

'Well, honey,' said Roxy, 'next time, I think I'd like to get a little of that sweetness too.' She glanced at Inga. 'Can't let Inga have all the fun.'

Inga smiled. 'And with a lovely cock that big, I think there's several ladies on board who would like to … as we say … receive some satisfaction.'

She winked at James, and then she and Roxy linked arms and turned for the door.

'We'll see you later, honey,' said Roxy over her shoulder.

And then they left, closing the door behind them.

James heard a click as the lock was fastened from the other side.

He let out a breath.

What. Was. That. All. About?

James realised that he was lying on the bunk completely naked, and so sat up and found his clothes. As he dressed, he wondered what this all meant. If he had been captured by pirates, why he was not dead, or swabbing decks, instead of getting his cock comprehensively sucked by a beautiful woman?

Given the circumstances, though, he was quite pleased with his position. Those girls had been insanely sexy, and they were promising more?

Well, bring it on!

James lay back down on the bunk and put his hands behind his head. He realised there was still some liquid in the goblet, so he sipped at it while his thoughts flew around all that had happened.

'It could be worse. A lot worse.'

7

On board the *Nancy*, Captain Bloodstock the Third peered through a secret spyhole into the cabin that the two English girls had been placed in.

They seemed okay, if a little confused as to why they were there and still alive.

Cradle admired the blonde one, the one called Charlotte. She was like a doll, with porcelain skin, and fine hair. She was very pretty, and he liked her small mouth and lips as well as her dainty hands, and her small waist, which was pinched into a night-corset.

The other girl, Molly, had dark hair, pinned up into a sensible bun. She was also pretty, but in a slightly harder way. Even if you didn't know, you would guess that Molly was used to hard work, whereas Charlotte's hands had probably only ever entered hot water in order to wash them.

He considered his options. He would have to try different approaches with the girls, he was sure, but first he would have to break them in gently, make them less afraid, and more willing to go along with whatever he had planned.

He smiled to himself. He would enjoy the challenge.

And watching how the girls responded and reacted.

He stepped away from the spyhole and headed to his own quarters, where two of his specially-trained female crew-members awaited. He intended to instruct them to prepare the girls for a party in about a week's time. At that party he would present the girls to his crew – and they would all be on their best behaviour throughout.

It had been a hard few months for them all, and they needed and deserved a break. And a party would be just the trick. A special pirate party.

Charlotte was staring out of the porthole at the sea when the door clicked behind her. She spun round to see a girl standing there. She was wearing a simple wrap, and was smiling.

Charlotte turned, and saw that Molly was watching carefully from her bunk.

'Hello?' said Charlotte hesitantly.

The girl smiled. 'You're to come with me,' she said. 'Both of you.'

'Where to?' asked Molly.

The girl looked at Molly. 'You must be in need of a bath?' she said. 'Follow me.'

The two girls followed the newcomer out of the room and down a short passageway. She led them into another room further along. There was no way to make a run for it. Charlotte looked for any possible way she and Molly might get out, but there were no other doors, and the room they had been in was at the end of a deck. So they had no real option but to follow the new girl.

The room they were shown to was slightly larger than the cell. It had a large copper bath on one side, which was already filled with steaming hot water. On the other side were a couple of raised platforms with towels thrown over them. Also in the room was a second girl, dressed again in a simple wrap. She smiled as they entered.

'You poor things,' she said. 'You must be exhausted.' She gestured to the bath. 'There's a nice hot bath for you both, and then we'll see about a massage to soothe those muscles.'

Charlotte and Molly watched as the two girls gave them towels and showed them where their clothes could be folded and placed.

The first girl tested the water with her hand, and smiled. 'It's good and ready.' She reached for a small glass jug and poured something into the water. It steamed and spread over the surface, and Charlotte could smell lavender and another, deeper, musky scent. It was most pleasant and inviting.

The two girls left the room, locking the door behind them, and Charlotte and Molly were left alone.

'This is … interesting …' said Molly. 'They clonk us on the head, kidnap us, lock us in a room, and then give us a hot bath. Very strange.'

Charlotte looked at the bath. 'It does look very nice, though,' she commented.

Molly nodded. 'Shame to waste it,' she said. 'Come on then. In for a penny …'

Molly started stripping off her clothes, and Charlotte watched in amazement as the girl removed everything, revealing a toned body, small pert breasts, and boyish hips.

'You just gonna stand there and let this bath go to waste?' said Molly. ''Coz I sure ain't.'

She stepped into the steaming water and gave a moan of pleasure. 'Oh, that's lovely.'

Charlotte watched as the girl sat and sank down into

the hot water with a big smile on her face.

Charlotte slowly unbuttoned her nightshift. She wasn't used to undressing in front of anyone, but she guessed she didn't have much choice.

She hung the shift over a nearby chair, and undid the stays on her night corset. Molly moaned again in the bath, luxuriating in the hot, oiled water.

Charlotte took off the rest of her clothes, folded and laid them on the chair, and then stepped into the bath with Molly.

The water felt amazing. It was hot and steaming, and the scented oils flew across the surface, coating her skin where they touched it.

She sat down opposite Molly, and they arranged their legs so they were side by side. It felt so good to be in the water. She sighed and laid her head back on the side of the bath. Her full breasts floated slightly in front of her, and she flapped the water over them.

'What do you think will happen to us, Molly?' she asked.

Molly grinned. 'I've no idea. But I've a feeling that it may depend on how much we want to enjoy it as it happens.'

'What do you mean?' asked Charlotte.

'Well,' Molly looked at Charlotte. 'It … I suppose it depends …'

'Depends on what?'

'Well …' Molly was embarrassed. 'Well, let me ask … have you been with a man before?'

Charlotte looked puzzled for a moment, and then her eyes opened wide.

'Molly!' she said, partly in shock and partly amused. She splashed some water over at Molly. 'How can you ask such a thing?'

Molly smiled, and then looked serious again. 'I'm serious, Charlotte,' she said. 'Have you?'

'Well ...' Charlotte blushed. 'Well, I'd never have told Mamma ... but ... there was this one boy ...'

Molly nodded, encouraging her to continue.

'It was nothing, really,' said Charlotte. 'But we did ... make love ... one time.'

'So you're not a virgin?' asked Molly.

'No ... no I'm not,' said Charlotte, playing with the water with her hand. 'What about you?'

Molly erupted into raucous laughter, and Charlotte wondered what she had said to cause such mirth. Eventually Molly calmed down, and stroked Charlotte's foot under the water.

'Oh, Charlotte,' she said. 'No, I'm not a virgin either ... I'm actually not a virgin a great many times.'

It was Charlotte's turn to giggle. The two girls laughed together then, and relaxed in the hot water.

'What did you mean, then, that it *depended*?'

Molly looked at her seriously. 'Charlotte. We are here, possibly alone, on a pirate ship. And if pirates are anything like they are reputed to be, then two young girls taken captive are unlikely to stay virgins for long, assuming they are virgins in the first place ... If you see what I'm saying?'

Charlotte's eyes grew wide. 'You mean ...'

'Yes,' nodded Molly. 'We might need to join in a little, in order to stay alive.'

Charlotte's eyes grew wider still as the meaning of Molly's words sank in. Molly, on the other hand, lay back with a faint smile on her face. It seemed that she was totally comfortable with their predicament, whereas for Charlotte, it was starting to feel very strange indeed. She swallowed, and rubbed the oily water over her body, absent-mindedly washing herself as her mind absorbed what she had learned.

She found herself washing and touching between her legs, the hair there rubbing through her fingers. She stopped, and looked at Molly to see if she had noticed, but Molly had her eyes closed and was apparently snoozing in the tub.

Charlotte sighed, and tried to relax. They would find out soon enough what these people had planned for them. She just hoped that she could manage to maintain some degree of dignity and decorum along the way.

Molly lay in the water, luxuriating in the warmth and the scents. She knew that Charlotte was inexperienced in sex, whereas she had enjoyed many lovers over the last few years. The prospect of ending up as some pirate wench sort of appealed to her … but she was concerned about her new friend.

She had watched Charlotte as she had undressed and got in the water, and her body was amazing. Full and sensual, her breasts bobbed in front of her as though they had some sort of hidden support, and her waist was tiny, even without the corsets. She had a down of blonde hair between her legs, and her whole demeanour was of a very sexy blonde angel, sent to give pleasure … but she doubted that Charlotte saw it this way. The girl seemed oblivious to her own body, the way she looked, and what that might stir in certain men …

Molly knew that she could look after herself, but that Charlotte might need a little guidance along the way. She resolved in her mind to do what she could for the girl. After all, they were in this – whatever *this* was – together.

8

There was a knock on the door, and Charlotte and Molly were startled out of their individual reveries.

'Erm … come in?' called Charlotte tentatively, and the door opened to reveal the same two girls as had led them to the room originally.

'We're just checking you're ready to come out now?' said one of the girls.

Molly and Charlotte exchanged glances, and Molly nodded. 'Yes … yes we are.'

'Excellent,' said the other girl, and the two picked up some fresh towels and held them out so that the two girls could step out of the bath and be wrapped up.

In the relative cool of the room, both Charlotte and Molly shivered slightly, and this was noted by their attendants.

'Not to worry,' said the first girl. 'Hop on this table here,' she indicated one of the raised benches on the other side of the room. 'We'll soon have you nice and warm again.'

Molly and Charlotte were led to the two tables, and clambered up onto them.

The second girl went over to a dresser at the side of

the room and returned with two small glasses of a dark liquid.

'Here you go,' she said. 'Drink up. This will warm you.'

'What is it?' asked Charlotte, taking one of the glasses in her hand.

'Rum,' said the girl. 'Perfect for an after-bath glow.'

Charlotte sniffed the drink carefully.

Molly took the other glass, and after smelling it, said, 'Well, bottoms up!' and downed the contents in one go.

Charlotte shrugged. If Molly could do it … She also downed the glass, and immediately coughed as the alcohol burnt down her throat.

The first girl, who was looking after Charlotte, patted and stroked her back. 'It gets better with practice,' she said. 'Now lie down.'

Charlotte lay on the table face down, her head turned so she could see Molly taking the same position on the other table. She smiled nervously.

'It will be okay,' said Molly. 'Trust me.'

'Now,' said the second girl, 'just relax and enjoy.'

Molly lay on the table, and the second girl gently stroked her back, then reached over and poured an amount of oil into her cupped palm.

'This might be a little cold,' she said, and tipped the oil onto Molly's shoulders and down her back.

It wasn't cold, but warm, and the oil was then quickly rubbed into Molly's skin.

Molly sighed. This was actually very nice! Her attendant's hands were strong, and they massaged all the right places down her spine, around her shoulders and upper arms.

More oil was added, and the massage continued down each leg, the muscles of the calves and feet being gently rocked and manipulated by the girl's hands.

When the girl reached her feet, Molly thought she had gone to heaven. The feeling of strong thumbs pressing the sensitive points in her feet brought pleasure all over her body. She felt herself relaxing even further.

There was a gentle moan from Charlotte, and Molly opened her eyes to see that her new friend was getting the same treatment, and that it was having a similar effect.

The massage continued up her legs, and Molly felt like she could lie here forever.

Then the strong hands reached her ass, and she felt them removed for a moment as more warm oil was poured over her cheeks. She felt it run in hot rivulets down her skin, over her bottom and down across her pussy.

The hands started their gentle massage again, pressing against the flesh of her bottom, and around to her upper thighs, where they moved between her legs and then up and around again.

The motion was strangely hypnotic, and Molly relaxed into it, enjoying the sensation of her flesh being moved and rubbed.

Across from Molly, Charlotte was also having her skin rubbed and manipulated by her attendant. She had never experienced anything quite like this before. The sensations were exquisite, and she felt more relaxed than she had for a long time.

The skilful hands were now concentrating on her bottom, rubbing the warm oil in and around and around.

Charlotte sighed and let herself go with the movement.

The hands moved around in circles, and Charlotte realised that the thumbs were starting to press against her little ass hole on each turn. And then, lower, her pussy lips were being gently stroked on each lower movement.

She squirmed a little, and the girl looking after her paused and rubbed her hand over her back again.

'It's okay,' she whispered. 'This is something that is required, to ensure that everything is in order.'

Charlotte nodded as best she could. 'O-okay,' she said.

'Don't worry,' whispered the girl. 'I won't do anything you don't want me to.'

The clever hands resumed their movements on her ass cheeks and around her thighs.

Charlotte found herself anticipating the movements, and as the thumbs brushed over her secret hole, she found herself pushing back slightly. Then, when they stroked down either side of her pussy, she again squirmed gently. The motion was starting to get to her, and she felt a distinct tingling in her nether regions.

More oil was added, and the two thumbs returned to around her asshole. They gently stroked around and around, and then one dipped a little deeper, making Charlotte gasp.

'Is that okay?' whispered the attendant girl. 'Should I continue?'

'Yes,' said Charlotte, not quite sure what she was agreeing to, but conscious too that saying 'No' might bring punishment.

The thumbs started to move in unison then, both dipping deeper and gently stretching her asshole as the moved. More oil was added, and Charlotte found herself writing gently and moaning as the thumbs worked her around and around and around.

Molly was getting the same treatment. And when she heard the furtive whisperings and then Charlotte start to moan in pleasure, this triggered something in her.

Her own attendant was working both her asshole and her pussy, the clever fingers, slick with oil, pressing down on her and making her own juices flow.

She glanced up at the girl who was working her, need in her eyes. The girl looked at her and smiled. She could see and tell that this one was more experienced, and could be taken a little further on this occasion.

'What do you need?' she whispered to Molly.

Molly swallowed. 'Something …' she managed to say, and then relaxed and tensed again as waves of pleasure washed over her from the manipulation.

'Just relax,' came the voice again. 'I have what you need.'

Molly tried to relax, and felt something firm press against her anus. She squirmed and felt it pop inside her. She had a rush of sensation as she realised that a small butt plug had been inserted into her. She felt full, but small electric sparks were kicking off inside her pussy.

The hands returned there, stroking her more intimately now. The thumbs gently spreading her, while clever fingers massaged her inner lips and clitoris.

She cried out in pleasure as the first thrum of an orgasm rippled through her. The hands relaxed their movement slightly, and let her recover, and then they were back, probing deeper, stroking her inner walls and making her so, so wet.

There was a movement in her ass, and the plug was

gently pushed again, allowing another, slightly bigger ridge to pop inside her.

Molly was starting to lose herself. The sensations and pleasure were overwhelming. She was moaning and squirming rhythmically in time with the girl's ministrations, the sensations and pressure building and growing.

Charlotte opened her eyes when she heard Molly cry out. She saw her companion lying there on her front, hands clenching the towel under her, as the girl looking after her moved her hands in and around and under her private parts.

Charlotte couldn't quite believe what she was seeing. Molly seemed to have some sort of flexible rod in her ass. As she watched, the attendant twisted it gently, and pushed it a little further in. The reaction from Molly was instantaneous: moaning and writhing and obviously enjoying it so, so much.

The hands on her own nether regions were continuing to stroke and manipulate her, and Charlotte realised that she was becoming very turned on at the sight and sound of Molly being expertly pleasured.

The girl looking after Charlotte saw that she was looking at Molly, and paused.

'Would you like what your friend is getting?'

Charlotte was startled by the question. Molly was obviously having the best experience here, but Charlotte was not sure.

She watched Molly. The girl's hands were moving faster under her now, and Molly was arching her back. Her face was clenched in pleasure, and Charlotte heard her hiss, 'Oh God, yes, yes, yes!' before she shuddered and moaned and was obviously having the most intense orgasm.

The girl servicing her slowed her movements, and allowed Molly to rest back on the bench. There was a happy smile on Molly's face.

'I think so,' said Charlotte.

Her attendant reached for the oil, poured more onto her ass, and started massaging her bottom once more, this time the thumbs moving deeper and deeper.

Charlotte wondered what she had let herself in for.

9

Captain Mirabella listened carefully as her two crew members reported back on their experience with James.

She nodded as they explained that he had cum early – the intense sensations being a little too much for him – but that they thought there was much potential, and that with training, he could be very serviceable indeed.

'Tell me again about his nipples,' said Mirabella.

'They were very sensitive,' said the first girl, Inga.

'He certainly enjoyed having them touched,' said Roxy.

Mirabella smiled thoughtfully. She had heard of a training method whereby a man could be encouraged to last longer, and to allow his release only on some pre-determined trigger. It was a little like the conditioning that some animals went through in order to make them obey … and Mirabella liked the idea of James being obedient.

She dismissed Inga and Roxy and, pouring herself a drink from a decanter, lay on her bed, deep in thought. She sipped her drink and idly ran her hand over her velvet leggings. Then she smiled, and sent for her cabin girl. There were plans to be made. Perhaps this James would enjoy what she had in mind … perhaps not. It would be interesting to find out.

Unaware of the plotting that was happening elsewhere on the ship, James lay on his bunk and looked at the ceiling. There was little else for him to do. No books had been provided, and his little cell-like room had no porthole or other means of seeing outside. So he was bored to tears.

His mind ran over his encounter with the two girls again and again, trying to make sense of it.

Who were they? Why had they come to him like that? Where was he? And what was going to happen to him?

Some food and a flagon of warm wine had been brought for him earlier, so he wasn't hungry or thirsty. Hopefully this meant that they didn't intend to kill him … but he wasn't sure. He was a little scared by it all, but was determined not to let this show.

He considered that if he played along with whatever these people wanted, then he might get a chance to escape … and that if he complained and struggled and was generally unhelpful, then they might think he wasn't worth the bother and dispose of him over the side of the ship.

He knew he was on a ship, as he could feel the movement in the boards. There was also the gentle hum of the waves as the vessel moved through them.

But as to where he was and where the ship was heading, he had no clue. He didn't even know what time it was; but he slept when he got tired, ate when he was hungry, and drank when he was thirsty.

It was all so monotonous and boring.

There was a gentle click over by the door, and it

swung open to reveal another girl. She was carrying a bundle of some sort, and behind her was a somewhat burly man, arms covered with tattoos. As James watched, the man folded his arms together and stood there like a rock. He was obviously there to ensure that James didn't try anything.

The girl smiled at him.

'Hi, I'm Lucy,' she said, and stepped forward into the room.

'Hello,' said James, eyeing her suspiciously.

She smiled at him. 'Don't worry, I'm not going to hurt you.'

She moved over to the table and placed the bundle there. She unwrapped it to reveal a pot, which she picked up and sniffed.

'It's not unpleasant,' she said. 'Here.'

She offered the pot to James, and he sniffed it cautiously. It did indeed have a pleasant smell. Musky and with a hint of cinnamon.

James sat up on his bunk and put his feet down on the floor.

What's was this all about?, he wondered. What were his captors up to? He wondered if this girl intended to fuck him as well … She was certainly pretty.

Lucy had long, curly brown hair that cascaded down her back. She seemed to be in her twenties, with clear skin and a twinkle in her eyes. She was wearing a tight jerkin that pushed her small breasts together, and a pair of brown leggings tucked into some black boots. All in all, she was very easy on the eye.

'What do you want?' James asked.

'The Mistress has asked that we begin your preparation,' said Lucy.

James frowned. 'The Mistress? Who is that?'

'Oh, she's the one in charge here. Don't worry. She doesn't intend you any harm. Quite the opposite, in fact. She has taken a shine to you.'

James didn't know what to make of that. But at least one thing seemed clear – he wasn't in any immediate danger.

James's mind settled on the other thing that Lucy had said. 'What preparation? What are you going to do?'

Lucy grinned at him, the twinkle back in her eye. 'It will be fine,' she said, 'and I promise you will enjoy it.'

James nodded hesitantly, not quite sure where this was all going. His eyes flicked to the man standing impassively in the doorway. There was no escaping that way.

Lucy saw James look at the man. 'Abdul,' she said, and the man turned his back on them. Still standing in the doorway, arms folded, an impassable barrier to whatever was down that passageway.

'Now then.' Lucy turned to James. 'What should I call you?'

James was a little tongue-tied. 'Erm … well … My name is James,' he said.

'James.' The girl smiled. 'James. Well, James, could I ask you to remove your britches, please, and lie back.'

'You want me to …?'

'Yes,' nodded Lucy. 'Well, I can't start the preparation if you're fully clothed, now can I?'

James could sense the flimsy logic there, and with a glance around the room, realised that he really had little choice. He stood and unbuttoned his britches, removing them and placing them on the floor by the cot.

Lucy smiled. 'That's good. Now if you could unbutton your shirt and lie back.'

James did as he was told. This was a little like the

checks they were given by the ship's nurse for ticks or head lice. A simple look-over to make sure they were clean. Maybe this Mistress wanted no infestations on her ship …

Lucy admired James's body. She could see why the Mistress liked this one so much. He had a lot of potential.

She stroked her hand down his chest, noting that his penis was small and flaccid. Well, she would do something about that.

James lay back and enjoyed the sensation of Lucy's hand trailing down his chest. He drew in a breath when her cool fingers found his penis, and gently stroked it, her fingers cupping his balls and massaging them slowly.

'Okay,' said Lucy. 'Let's begin.'

She picked up the pot and dipped her fingers in. They came out covered in a pale liquid, and she moved them together through it.

'This is a special concoction created by the Mistress's apothecaries. It's a combination of herbs and oils, and is guaranteed to have a very pleasing effect.'

She returned to James, and smeared some of the unguent onto his stomach. James could feel a gentle heat radiate from the area she touched. Not unpleasant or burning, just a very slight warming.

Lucy moved her hands, and as one cupped his penis, the other started to lather and massage the ointment into his cock. The effect was almost immediate.

James started as he felt the warming sensation spread down his loins and up his cock. He sensed his arousal starting, and swallowed, throwing his head back on the pillow as Lucy slowly massaged his cock, which was growing with every stroke.

Lucy smiled as she saw the effect she was having. James's penis was growing steadily. She could feel it hardening in her hands, growing longer and firmer.

She massaged his balls again and felt them tightening as the blood rushed to his cock. The head of his penis was starting to emerge from his foreskin.

She stroked her hand up his cock and rubbed gently at the point that the foreskin joined the head. James jerked gently, unable to prevent his body from reacting to a touch on that sensitive point. Lucy continued gently to massage the head of his cock, now fully emerged from its sheath and reaching full hardness.

Lucy ran both hands down James's cock, which was now around eight inches long, and straining. She could feel the veins in the sides, and slight pressure from her thumbs showed that the member was now strong and hard in her hands.

James was starting to breathe heavily. The whole of his nether regions were now tingling and burning in a most pleasurable way. Whatever was in that ointment was certainly working on him.

He remembered the girls from earlier, and his slight mishap as he had peaked too early, and momentary panic crossed his face. He could feel himself building and building, and he was sure it wouldn't be long …

He moaned as Lucy again stroked the full length of his engorged cock, her hand slick with the oil. Her clever fingers stroked around the head before her palm stroked back down to the base again.

Her other hand was cupping his balls, weighing them in her hand and providing support for his cock.

Lucy smiled at James when she saw his pained expression. 'Don't worry,' she said. 'You are going to enjoy this.'

She frowned a little and returned her concentration to her hands. She gripped his shaft a little firmer, and started a series of strokes up and down, which sent off fireworks in James's head. The sensations were amazing.

His cock jerked and jumped, and his legs started to twitch as the girl expertly wanked him with her hand. Slow and then fast, caressing and stroking, pausing at the top stroke to touch his sensitive glans, and then back down again to where her other hand was massaging his balls and the bottom of his shaft.

James moaned again, and Lucy looked appraisingly at his face. She could sense that he was close, but the purpose of this treatment was not for him to explode. In fact, it was the exact opposite … It was to make him hold back, to increase his staying power, and to allow him release only when she wanted it.

She sped up the movements of her hand, and James tensed his whole body in pleasure. As he started to reach his peak, Lucy kept her hands at the base of his penis and gently squeezed there, stopping his orgasm in its tracks. James's cock jerked and spasmed, but with Lucy in charge, there was nothing he could do but return from the plateau he had climbed, and lie there panting on the bed, still hard as a rock and still unfulfilled.

'That's excellent,' crooned Lucy. 'A few more like that, and you'll be well on your way.'

James wasn't listening. Lucy had started moving her hands again, and he was quickly ascending the peak once more. He could hear her whispering to him, something about obeying the Mistress, but her words were being lost in the rush of sensation from his groin. She moved her hand faster and faster, and then, just as James was about to reach the point of no return, she stopped, returned her hand to the base, gently squeezing to stop his pleasure once more.

James moaned in pleasure, his hands clutching the blanket on his cot.

Once more Lucy started to move her hand, and James stiffened, crying out as the pleasure peaked fast now. Lucy stopped moving and squeezed again, a small smile playing over her lips.

James thrashed his head from side to side. It wasn't fair. He'd usually have cum by now, and the tormenting, slick sensation of the girl's hand on his engorged cock, combined with the gentle tingling heat from the oils, was driving him mad. He couldn't think straight, and all his sensation was focused on his dick and the hand that was stroking him again … and again … and again.

Lucy released his cock and it sprung to attention, bobbing in the air, the head engorged with blood and throbbing. She gently stroked it with her fingers, eliciting a loud moan from James.

He was nearly ready.

She took some more of the oil from the pot and gently spread it over his cock. It was clever stuff. Designed both to stimulate and to hold back the release. Whenever she used it, she got very good results.

Lucy squeezed her legs together gently. Playing with a lovely big cock like this always got her hot, but this was work and not pleasure. She smiled as she ran her hand again over a moaning James's member, thinking that she would like to be fucked by this young man at some point … but not now. Once he had been trained and could stay the distance, then he would be a joy to ride and fuck until she was in a blissful state similar to that into which she had put him. She remembered her own training, how she had been stimulated while the Mistress's attendants had whispered words of submission and compliance into her ears. She never remembered what they had said, but the words had embedded themselves deep in her subconscious, ensuring that she would become exactly what the Mistress wanted her to be.

For the moment, though, she would have to content herself with one of the other slaves. She looked forward to the time, later on, when she would choose one from the deck, take him back to her room and get him to pleasure her. She would deserve it after her work here.

James continued to moan and thrash on the bed. The sensations over and around his cock and balls were intense now, and he found that although he was peaking and spasming almost constantly, he could not cum. A part of his mind wanted to so badly, but something was holding him back.

The gentle whispering in his ear stopped, and he realised, coming down from another pre-orgasmic high, that Lucy had ceased her ministrations on his cock. He opened his eyes and looked at her with yearning. At that moment she was the most beautiful thing he had ever seen, and he needed release so badly.

He lifted his arm and tried to touch her, but she moved out of his way. His arm and hand fell back to the cot, and he moaned in frustration. His hand moved to his cock and gently touched it. It was so hard and so sensitive. He stiffened as his hand moved around his own cock and stroked it gently. Oh, that was so good.

'Do you want me to release you?' Lucy smiled and looked into James's eyes.

James looked back, not sure what she meant, but wanting anything to release him from this orgasmic thrall in which he was held. He nodded.

Lucy nodded back. 'There is something … something that will release you.'

'Anything,' croaked James.

Lucy leaned a little closer. 'It will work every time,' she whispered, 'but you will find, in time, that it is the only thing that will work.'

Lucy knew that this was the key to training James, to get him to comply and to be able to perform as and when the Mistress required.

She reached out her hand and stroked his cock once more, feeling it jerk and stiffen again with her touch. He was so close …

She leant over and gently kissed James's stomach, stroking his cock with her hand. She moved her head up his body, planting a row of kisses. James squirmed in pleasure at what her hand was doing to him.

When Lucy reached his chest, she looked up at his face. 'This is what you need,' she said, and bent her head to his nipple, which was firm and standing erect.

She teased it with her lips and the tip of her tongue, and then suckled it gently, playing with it with her teeth.

All the time, her hand stroked James's cock firmly, keeping him on the plateau of pleasure to which she had brought him.

James was in heaven. He had fireworks going off in his head. His cock was being stroked firmly, and the sensations of his nipple being teased sent him over the edge.

'Oh … oh … *Oh* …' he cried out as the clever hand stroked him, and her lips and tongue played with his nipple.

His cock leaked pre-cum from the end, and Lucy ran her thumb over it and massaged it in. She continued her teasing rhythm, feeling James's breathing start to get ragged.

Suddenly he was there, and she removed her lips

from his nipple as his cock shot a stream of semen up into the air. She continued to work his cock as more cum bubbled from the end and ran back down the shaft.

James was tensing and moaning as he came. The relief was immense, and he cried out as he ejaculated over and over as Lucy's hand worked him.

He shuddered, and she slowed her movements, allowing him to come back down to reality, her hand stroking him gently. Eventually she slowed her movements and just held his cock at its base, letting the cum slowly run down and pool around it.

'Are you okay?' she asked.

James opened his eyes and blurrily looked at her. He smiled. 'I'm … I'm fine,' he said with a smile.

Lucy nodded and released his cock. Even though he had cum, it was still hard and firm. A further property of the oil; and something James would learn had its advantages too.

Lucy stood and moved over to where James's bowl of washing water stood. She cleaned her hands with a rough piece of soap, and dried them on James's towel. When she had finished, she picked up the pot of oils and recorked it, wrapping it in her own towel once more.

'You'll have more sessions like that,' she said. 'Hope that's okay.'

'Do I have any choice?' said James.

Lucy smiled. 'No, not really. Until next time.'

She turned and left the room, the large tattooed man walking in front of her. She closed the door behind her, and James heard the key click in the lock.

He was alone again, lying partly naked on his bed, semen pooling around his erect cock, and with a silly smile on his face.

10

The time passed slowly for Charlotte and Molly. Each day fell into the same pattern for them.

They would wake, wash and then wait for the attendants to arrive for their morning session. This usually involved a massage or a bath in scented oils, and the attendants would ensure that their intimate parts were teased and manipulated until they were so turned on that they could barely control their desires.

Then they would be dressed in some loose clothing and given some wine and food – usually some bread and cheese, nothing too fancy. Then, after eating, they would rest until the attendants returned once again to train them in various ways.

Charlotte was starting to enjoy herself, and while she wondered what had become of her Mother and sister, she was becoming quite caught up in her own sexual desires and the power that they brought her.

Molly, on the other hand, was completely revelling in the opportunity to try as many different sexual experiences as she could. The attendants had used a variety of devices on her, and she had enjoyed them all. The massage and gentle stretching that her ass had received ensured that now she could accommodate a butt plug of the widest girth that they had, and she squealed with delight as they slowly slid the oiled object into her, twisting it to give her the most amazing sensations.

Charlotte was not quite so enthusiastic. She wasn't keen on having her ass violated, and so the attendants, strangely compliant to what she wanted, concentrated instead on her pussy and breasts. She had found that she took a certain enjoyment from having her nipples pinched. The sharp pain provided an erotic counterpart to the sensations of her pussy being filled with a hard dildo. She wondered what all this might mean, and, indeed, where it was all leading.

After about a week of all this primping and training, the two girls were starting to get a little nervous about the party they were expected to attend. The serving girl who regularly brought them their food and drink had mentioned the event to them, and had seemed impressed that they would be going. Molly had tried to quiz her further on who was behind all this, but all she had managed to obtain was a name: Captain Bloodstock. What this Captain's intentions were, and what he hoped to achieve by keeping them captive and subjecting them to all this sexual pleasure and training, was unknown.

Of course, both girls had an idea as to where this might all end … slavery. They realised that the one thing pirates ultimately wanted was money – the chance to make a quick sale – so it wasn't a huge leap to assume that the two of them were being prepared for sale, possibly auction, to some rich man somewhere, to serve as his concubines.

The idea filled Charlotte with dread. She had never thought that her life would be mapped out in this way. She had her heart set on meeting a handsome army captain or soldier who would whisk her off her feet, marry her and then keep her in a luxurious house in the country somewhere, full of billowing curtains and gold cutlery.

Molly however was less reserved. Her life to date had been one of servitude – although not much hardship, if she was honest, as the *Providence* had afforded her a higher standard of living than some servants she had heard of. But she was still apprehensive as to what would become of them. She was also feeling quite protective toward Charlotte, recognising that the other girl was not as experienced as she, and thus suffering a little at the indignities they were being put through.

Then, one day, there was a departure from their usual routine.

Charlotte yawned and stretched.

The girls had been woken as usual by the sunlight streaming through the porthole in their room, and also by the sounds of raised voices up on deck.

'It's today, isn't it?' said Molly.

Charlotte frowned. 'Today? Oh goodness.' Her face crumpled in an expression of terror.

Molly moved to sit beside her friend. 'It will be all right, Charlotte. I'll look after you.'

Charlotte rested her head on Molly's shoulder and closed her eyes. The panic subsided. She was happy that Molly was there, to be honest. At least she wasn't completely alone in this … whatever it was.

There was a click at the door, and it opened to reveal someone bringing their morning food and drink. But it wasn't the usual servant girl who stood there. Instead, it was a taller woman with long, curly dark hair that fell down her back. She was carrying their tray, but at her waist was a black leather belt on which hung a cutlass. Her legs were clad in a deep purple velvet material that clung tightly to her thighs, and from her feet to her knees were a pair of black leather boots with impressively high heels. Her top was a simple peasant blouse, but over that she wore a leather jerkin studded with metal pins. Her arms were bare, and Molly noted that they were well toned and muscled.

The woman moved into the room, and Charlotte observed that although there was another girl with her, she remained outside the door, guarding against any attempt to escape.

The woman placed the food and water down on a table and then turned to face them as they sat together on the bed. She looked from one to the other, studying them intently. Her eyes twitched and narrowed as she took in their simple nightshifts, and the curves of their bodies beneath.

'So,' she said eventually. 'You are the girls.'

Charlotte and Molly looked at one another briefly, not sure how to respond.

The woman smiled, and it was not a nasty smile. They could feel a warmth coming from her, which they hadn't felt from the two female attendants who had been seeing to them each day.

'How have you been looked after?' asked the woman, looking at each of them in turn. 'Have you been fed and watered?'

'Um,' said Charlotte, 'yes … yes we have.'

The woman nodded. 'And what of your treatment, has that been to your satisfaction?'

Molly smiled. She remembered the many, many orgasms, the caressing and oiling, the intense and sustained pleasure … She looked at the woman, who was regarding her quizzically. 'Yes, yes it has all been … most pleasurable.'

'But where are we?' blurted out Charlotte.

The woman turned her gaze to the blonde girl and eyed her up and down.

Mirabella could see that this one was the more inexperienced and afraid. She had asked Captain Bloodstock if she could check in on the girls that he had chosen, in exchange for him seeing her own boy. Cradle had been reluctant at first, but after a little … persuasion … he had agreed. Mirabella always liked the persuasion … most pleasurable.

These two certainly looked as though they had potential. Mirabella was impressed. Cradle had chosen well.

'My dear,' said Mirabella. 'Why don't you know where you are?'

Charlotte swallowed. She had no idea who this woman was, or what she wanted, but this was an opportunity to speak to someone other than the female attendants they usually saw. And she seemed interested in their predicament.

'We were kidnapped,' she said. 'Taken from my family and my ship. We've been kept here ever since.'

The woman frowned. 'Kidnapped,' she said. 'Surely not.'

Charlotte started to speak, but noticed a small smile playing at the corner of the woman's mouth. She was enjoying this. Charlotte stopped speaking.

Molly watched the exchange. She had met many, many nobles and members of the gentry over the years she had been working on the *Providence*, and had a pretty good idea about what sort of people they were from the moment they first opened their mouths. This woman was dressed well, expensively even – leather boots like those did not come cheap – and her whole attitude was one of superiority.

'It's you who took us,' Molly said.

Charlotte looked at Molly, her eyes wide.

'Admit it,' said Molly.

The woman smiled. 'Well, actually, I didn't.'

Molly looked at her.

'It's true,' the woman insisted. 'I didn't take you.'

'Well, if you didn't, then who did?' asked Charlotte. 'We've no idea as to who has done this or why.'

The woman looked at them both and smiled again. 'At least you are well,' she said. 'And I understand you have a party to attend tomorrow night …'

Molly exchanged a glance with Charlotte. So, the party was not that evening, but the next. 'Do you know what happens at this party?' she asked. She was still concerned that they might be auctioned off to the highest bidder.

'Fun,' said the woman. She gave a final smile and stood. 'I won't be there on this occasion – I have something of my own to occupy me – but I am assured that you girls will have a great time.'

With that, she nodded to the girls, turned and left the room.

The attendant closed the door behind her, and they heard the key snick in the lock.

'What was all that about?' asked Charlotte.

'I have no idea,' said Molly.

James was lying on his bunk. His mind, however, was full of thoughts about what the next session with Lucy might bring.

Over the last few days, she had visited him twice a day, and on each occasion she had brought him to the peak of ecstasy time and again, keeping him hanging and wanting to cum so badly. But she would not let him touch her. Nor would she do any more than stimulate his cock with her clever hands and nails, kissing his body and whispering in his ear as he writhed in pleasure under her ministrations.

What he had noticed was that his staying power had increased. From that initial assignation with the two girls – and try as he might, he could not remember their names – when he had exploded early, he was now able to keep hard for the entire duration. In fact, he could not cum at all until his nipples were teased and sucked. This fact was not lost on him, and the sensations associated with that were what he yearned for.

The previous night, long after Lucy had left, he had been lying in his bunk, replaying in his mind the activities he had enjoyed with her. He had found his cock stiffening, and before long, had been pumping it vigorously with his hand. In the past, it had taken only around a minute or two before he had been shooting all over the sheets, but last night he had wanked and wanked himself, feeling wave after wave of pleasure wash over him, but had been unable to cum. In the end he had simply given up, and slipped off to sleep with the biggest hard-on that he had ever had throbbing unfulfilled between his legs.

James smiled to himself and remembered the feeling of Lucy manipulating his cock, and it twitched in response.

He was just contemplating seeing if he could again try to pleasure himself to completion, when there was a click at the door as the key was turned. James jumped and hurriedly looked about the room. Everything was in place.

The door swung open, and James saw that one of his regular attendants had opened it. But behind him was another man, someone James hadn't seen before.

The man stepped forward and eyed James up and down. He cleared his throat.

'Are you being treated well?' he asked.

James was puzzled and a little wary. He nodded.

'Yes. Who are you?'

'I'm … Captain Bloodstock.'

'Why am I here?'

The Captain looked a little embarrassed, but took another step into the room.

'You being here is, I must confess, something to do with me, but I am not your captor. I needed to see that everything was good, however, and that you were being treated well by your hosts.'

James sat up in his bunk and pulled his trews toward him. This man, this Captain or whatever he was, had something to do with his imprisonment here …

'Why am I here?' he asked again, starting to pull his trews over his legs. The Captain watched him for a moment, and took a step back.

'I can't tell you that,' he said. 'But if you behave and do as instructed, then I can promise you that no harm will come to you.'

'What about my ship?' James asked. 'And all the passengers? What about them?'

The Captain was dismissive. 'They were … unharmed,' he said. 'We took what we wanted and left … No need for carelessness with the people. We need them to tell everyone what happened.'

James looked puzzled. 'But … what … who are you

people?'

The Captain smiled. 'Why … we are pirates!'

James was at a loss as to what to say.

Captain Bloodstock laughed. 'I can see by your face that this puzzles you, but don't worry. Pirate life can be very … enjoyable.'

He stepped back into the corridor, and James saw that Lucy was there also. She smiled at Bloodstock and stepped past him into the room.

'I shall see you later on,' said Bloodstock. 'I can see that you are fine, and well cared for … and I am told that things are progressing well … So, for now …' He performed an extravagant bow and turned.

Lucy shut the door behind him, and turned to James. 'So, James,' she said. 'Seems that I left you … in a little agitation last night.'

She smiled and glanced down, to where James's cock and balls were exposed as he was struggling to get his pants on.

'Let me help you with that.'

She approached him on the bunk and gently pushed him back. She kissed him gently, and James stopped struggling with his clothing, lay back, and allowed her cool hand to stroke down his stomach, around the base of his cock, and to hold his balls. His cock twitched in response and started to grow.

'That's my lovely boy,' murmured Lucy, letting her hand softly stroke his balls, cupping them gently.

James moaned as Lucy's head dipped and her lips fluttered over his nipple. Her tongue extended and licked around it, and his cock jumped in Lucy's hand.

Lucy smiled, and turned her attention to the other nipple, which brought the same abrupt stiffening of his cock. The training was progressing very well indeed.

She shifted her position and moved down James's body. He got more comfortable on the bunk, and she knelt between his legs and started to stroke his cock slowly up and down with her hands, while looking steadily into his eyes. Watching him twitch and move as she manipulated him.

'Did you have a hard night?' she crooned. 'Did we leave you all cocked and nowhere to go?'

James nodded and moaned again as she grazed the head of his penis with her lips, before suckling on it gently. All the time gently stroking and caressing his balls and shaft with her hands.

He was now rock hard, and he knew, ready to cum.

Lucy did not give James relief, though. She focused her attention on his shaft and balls, and stroked and caressed and licked them, making him shudder and moan with delight.

A bead of pre-cum emerged from the tip of his cock, and Lucy caught it on her tongue and spread it over the head, before gently suckling again at the spot where the head joined the shaft.

Lucy ministered to James's cock for some time, feeling it twitch and move, and listening to James moan and thrash under her. She so wanted to feel him inside her, but the Mistress had forbidden that for the moment. Lucy would have to take her own pleasure with the other men of the crew … and experiencing James would have to wait a while longer.

She looked up again at James's face, which was flushed in response to her expert movements. But he had not cum. Which was the whole point. She was good at her job.

'Now then,' she said, smiling at him. 'You've been such a good, good boy. Should I allow you to cum?'

Her words were ecstasy to James's ears. He nodded, eyes wide. 'Yes … yes …' he moaned.

'Yes what?' teased Lucy.

'Yes … mistress,' stammered James, knowing what she wanted to hear, and also knowing that he needed release. He needed to cum.

'Good boy,' whispered Lucy. With her hand still caressing his swollen cock, she moved her head up and captured his nipple between her lips. She swirled her tongue around it, and gently bit with her teeth.

James stiffened. He could feel electric shocks from his nipple to his cock, and felt the surge of pressure in his balls. As Lucy continued to manipulate his nipple with her tongue and teeth, and his cock with her hand, he stiffened and let out a strangled cry.

The pressure was coming … He stiffened his legs involuntarily. He could feel it … Yes … There was a moment of exquisite enjoyment, when he felt the barriers removed, and the next thing he knew was waves of pleasure running up and down his body. His skin became hyper-sensitive, and his nipples were erect and straining. And his cock …

Held in Lucy's hand, James's cock erupted with cum. The white fluid pumped from the end and ran down her hand, making it slick. She gripped a little harder and pumped him gently, smiling as he writhed in pleasure beneath her.

She loved having so much control over a man. In this state, a man would do anything, could not deny her anything, was totally hers.

She removed her lips from his over-sensitive nipple and moved her head up to his ear. She sucked the lobe into her mouth, and smiled around it as she saw a fresh eruption of cum from his cock spill down around her hand.

'You like this, James?' she whispered needlessly. 'You want more?'

James moaned and blinked. All he could think of was the intense pleasure that this woman was giving him. He moaned and said, 'Yes.'

'Good boy,' she whispered, and kissed his earlobe. 'Just remember what I can do for you.' She pumped his cock a little more, causing more cum to be forced from the end. 'Do what I say, and you can have more.'

James nodded. He would agree to anything.

Lucy smiled, and gently released his sticky cock, which was still hard and throbbing. But the initial pressure had been relieved. Now she would see how much longer she could keep him hard ... and maybe even reward him with another orgasm at the end ... Yes ... James's training was coming along very well indeed.

11

The next day, Molly and Charlotte were woken early. It was the day of the party, and both knew that it was special for them.

They were fed and given water to drink, and then both were taken to the bath to be cleaned and scrubbed and prepared for the evening's event.

'What do you think will happen?' asked Charlotte with a quaver in her voice. She was very nervous about what the coming hours might bring.

'No idea,' replied Molly from the other end of the bath. 'But I hope it will be enjoyable.'

A pair of maids tasked with washing the two girls ran soap over their upper bodies. Charlotte tensed as she felt her maid's hand pass over her breasts, her nipples erect at the sensation of being touched.

'You need to relax,' said her maid gently. She rubbed more soap over Charlotte's shoulders and sluiced it off with hot water. Charlotte smiled. She knew that the girl – one of several attendants who had been looking after them while they had been there – meant no harm.

Charlotte closed her eyes as the maid ran her hands over her body again, dipping below the water to her cleft. Her body tensed slightly in anticipation as the girl massaged her body. As she and Molly had been pampered and preened each day, so they had been manipulated sexually, bringing them often to intense pleasure, and now their bodies were well tuned to the sensations. Charlotte found herself craving the attention, longing to be stroked and massaged to orgasm.

Molly moaned loudly from her end of the bath, and Charlotte looked across to where her friend's attendant had her hand beneath the water, playing with Molly's most sensitive area.

'Oh God,' said Molly. 'I need something soon … These girls are driving me crazy!'

Charlotte frowned. 'You need …?' Her frown broke as she realised what Molly meant. The pleasuring they had received from the female attendants had been enjoyable, but had stirred in them a lust and longing for something more. Both girls were completely straight, and both were missing the attentions of the opposite sex. Stroking and caressing and licking were all very good, but sometimes a girl just needed a good hard cock to play with.

Charlotte got out of the bath, and allowed her maid to dry her carefully. Then she lay down on the low bed for further massage.

Molly splashed a little in the bath water, and cried out as she orgasmed from the hand that was working her. Her hands clutched the edge of the bath as she stiffened in pleasure.

Her attendant allowed her to calm a little, and then helped her out of the bath and onto another bed.

The two girls lay there looking at the wooden ceiling of the cabin. Their attendants turned to one of the tables that lined the edges of the room, and then returned, each holding a small jar of oils, and a sharp razor.

They bade the girls to relax, and then gently smoothed oil over their pubic regions, using the razors to take off the fine down that grew there. Charlotte had never shaved there before, and watched in amazement as her pink skin was revealed. The attendants expertly removed every trace of hair, then smeared on another unguent, which tingled slightly.

'This will stop any further growth for the moment,' Charlotte's attendant said. 'And it moisturises and nourishes the skin.'

Charlotte moved her hand down and stroked the skin of her pubis. It was incredibly soft and smooth, and she felt small electric shocks as she drifted her fingertips over the area. She wondered to herself what the purpose of this treatment was, but had a suspicion as to what the evening might bring.

Molly had received the same treatment, and was now lying back as her legs and arms were massaged.

The girls were happy and relaxed, and allowed the pleasure to wash over them, as massaging hands moved to their loins, stroking and encouraging them.

Charlotte cried out again as another orgasm rocked through her from what her attendant was doing. Her eyes were closed, and the pleasure rushed through her body.

Molly was close behind, and the sound of Charlotte crying in pleasure brought her to a peak too, and she hitched and rocked as the sensations overtook her.

Both girls breathed hard as their attendants slowed their movements, allowing them to recover. They were given soft towels to dry themselves with, and then left alone in the room.

Molly laughed. 'Sheesh … If that's what bath time is always like here, I'll have some more of that!'

Charlotte blushed. 'It was very … pleasant,' she said.

'Pleasant! You have a habit for understatement. That was amazing.'

Charlotte smiled. 'It was, wasn't it? I wonder what this party will be like?'

Molly grinned. 'As long as there are some nice fit blokes there … I don't think we'll really care, will we?'

Charlotte frowned momentarily. 'You think we will …?'

Molly nodded. 'I think that we will very much …'

She laughed again, and Charlotte couldn't help but smile too … What would the coming hours bring?

12

There was music playing as Molly and Charlotte were led into the ship's ballroom. The two girls were amazed to realise how large the ship actually was, as all they had seen before were the few rooms they had been allowed access to. But the place was enormous!

Off to one side were tables laden with food and drink. Platters of fruits and cheeses, meats and other sweets the likes of which they had never seen. There were whole legs of pork, with knives ready to slice the meat thickly or thinly, and smaller forks to eat with.

It was all quite civilised, and Molly and Charlotte looked around, taking in all the trappings of wealth and culture that they just hadn't expected from a pirate ship.

There were people there too. Pirates, they guessed; but there were men and women, all dressed in fine outfits. Most of the women wore gowns with low décolletage, the tops of their breasts glistening in the lamplight. The men wore breeches and shirts, coats and ruffles. Present on every person, however, were weapons. The men wore leather belts from which hung swords and cutlasses; the ladies had shorter knives and swords pushed through their belts, or held on leg-suspenders that peeked through the skirts as they moved.

The music was slow and hypnotic – a waltz of some sort – and some of the partygoers swayed together to the rhythm.

Charlotte and Molly wandered through a throng of people, and took up a position by one of the walls. They noticed in one corner at the back a closed door and, adjacent to that, four open windows, apparently leading to a small annexe beyond. Leaning into the ballroom through two of the windows were a couple of the women, visible only from the chest up. They were talking to each other, but every so often, one of them would shut her eyes, open her mouth and shudder gently, before the movement subsided and she returned to their conversation, slightly flushed.

Charlotte wondered what on earth was happening, but then Molly nudged her, and they both watched as an oiled slave, his skin as black as night, crossed the dancefloor and went through into the annexe, closing the door behind him. He was stripped to the waist, but the girls could see that beneath his loose pantaloons was a member of impressive size. It bulged his pants at the front, and the man was rubbing it gently as he went through the door.

Charlotte's eyes moved from where the man had gone, to the two women leaning out of the windows. One of the women moaned loudly, and shuddered, her hands clutching the windowsill. She was obviously having the most intense orgasm. She slowed her breathing, opened her eyes and smiled in a very languid and relaxed manner. She looked back and said something to someone behind her. Then she moved back and out of the window.

'What's happening there?' hissed Charlotte.

Molly was just looking amused. 'Keep watching the door,' she said.

Charlotte did as she said, and after a moment, the same woman appeared there in the doorway. She was still flushed, and as she left, her hand was taken by a different black man. He was slightly taller than the one they had seen go into the annexe, and his head was bald. He was also stark naked, and Charlotte's eyes widened when she saw his cock, semi-erect and hanging to his thigh.

'Oh my goodness,' she whispered.

'I know,' giggled Molly.

The man kissed the woman's hand gently, then went past her and disappeared into the annexe. The woman smiled, looked around her, and made her way unsteadily back into the party.

As the girls watched, another woman broke away from the people she was talking with and knocked on the door to the annexe. It was opened by the bald man, and she smiled broadly.

Moments later, she appeared at one of the windows, holding tight to the windowsill. She talked briefly to someone behind her, and then her eyes closed, and her mouth dropped open, as she started to rock gently.

After a minute or so, she shuddered and flushed bright red, her hands now clutching at the sill.

'I want some of that …' said Molly.

Charlotte's eyes widened. 'You mean, those men You want to …?'

'Yes indeed,' grinned Molly. 'After all, it is a party, and we were invited!'

Charlotte shook her head. 'Not for me … That man … he was so …'

'Big?' said Molly, raising an eyebrow. 'I bet it feels

amazing.'

Charlotte blushed. 'I … I'm a little hungry,' she said. 'I think I'll get some food.'

She moved across to where the tables of food were positioned. She selected a small plate, and added to it some of the meats and cheeses. Some grapes too, as she had always liked those. Then she turned and looked around for Molly.

That devil-girl, she had headed straight to the annexe entrance, where she was now deep in conversation with a large black man. Like the first they had seen, he was stripped to the waist, and Charlotte's eyes roamed over his muscled arms and torso. She shuddered a little, imagining what such a man could do.

She saw Molly raise her hand and gently stroke the man's arm, which looked massive against her petite fingers.

Molly glanced across to where Charlotte was standing, and shot her a grin. Then she disappeared through the doorway, pausing only briefly to let past the other of the two women they had first seen at the windows, who now exited the annexe and rejoined the party.

Charlotte looked quickly around to see if anyone had seen, but everyone else in the room was occupied with eating, drinking and chatting. No-one gave much mind to what was happening at the back.

Charlotte sighed to herself, and munched on a piece of cheese, wondering what Molly was getting herself into now.

As Molly's eyes adjusted to the subdued light beyond the door, she saw that the annexe was indeed much smaller than the main ballroom, but draped in sumptuous velvets and silks. There were four raised benches, only one of which was currently occupied. Each allowed a woman to position herself on all fours, leaning out of one of the windows that let onto the ballroom. Then there was a space behind for the men to stand in.

Molly watched as the woman they had just seen enter was expertly serviced by the large black man standing behind her.

His cock was jutting out in front of him, at least a foot long. It was gleaming with the woman's juices, and he thrust it smoothly into her vagina again and again.

She shuddered with every stroke, and the man held her hips steady as he started to increase his rhythm.

Suddenly she bucked on him and screamed as she came hard all over his cock. Her white juices coated the man's penis, and he slowed his pace a little as she shuddered and bucked under him.

When she had recovered, he started to fuck her hard again, causing her to cum once more …

Molly had a moment of worry – what had she got herself into? – before the man she was with took her by the hand and led her to one of the vacant benches. She moved behind it, and the man helped her rearrange her dress so that her privates would be fully exposed once she was positioned on it.

Then he helped her up, and she leaned out of the window, blinking in the oil light, and looking for Charlotte.

She made eye contact with her across the room, and smiled.

The man behind her stroked her bare arse. 'Let me know what you need, madame,' he said, his voice deep and rich like treacle.

Molly nodded back. 'Slow at first,' she said. 'Then fast

and hard …' She couldn't believe she had just asked for that …

The man nodded once, and started stroking Molly's arse cheeks, spreading them gently. She felt some oil being spread over them and gently rubbed into her aching pussy.

She looked across at Charlotte again, and saw that her friend was talking to one of the other pirates, who had just approached her. She locked eyes with her friend again, just as she felt the most enormous cock enter her from behind.

Her eyes closed in pleasure, as the immense weapon slid smoothly deep into her pussy, sending tingles of pleasure up her spine.

Then it slowly withdrew, and she could feel every vein, every part of the man's dick as it made its way back up into her body. Then it withdrew again, then thrust in again …

Oh my, she thought, *this is fucking good!*

The man was obviously an expert at this, and trained to understand the signs from the woman he was pleasuring. He slowly increased his pace, his cock thrusting a little deeper each time. Molly moaned and wiggled her bottom against him, and the pleasure built and built.

Suddenly, she was cumming all over the man's cock, crying out, as the pleasure shot all over her body, sending electricity running the length of her arms and legs. If she hadn't been supported so well on the couch, then her legs would have failed her. They felt like jelly!

The man asked 'More?' and Molly looked back and nodded once. She drew in a breath and held it momentarily as the man slowly thrust into her again, then started to speed up.

Molly lost all track of time, as she was professionally fucked for the first time in her life. He was magnificent. His large cock pounded into her again and again, drawing orgasm after orgasm from her. She moaned and writhed and cried out, but he didn't stop.

Eventually, he slowed, and Molly felt the stupidest smile cross her face. She was so replete. The man withdrew his cock from her pussy with a soft squelching sound, and she collapsed into the window frame with a happy sigh.

There was a smattering of applause, and she opened her eyes to see a group of the pirates standing watching her. They nodded to each other and complimented her performance. She smiled weakly, and let herself be helped down off the bench.

The large black man helped her adjust her clothing, and then took her hand.

'It was a pleasure to serve you, madame,' he rumbled.

Molly smiled at him. 'Why, thank you … What is your name?'

'Joachim, madame.'

'Joachim … I may ask for you again …' She gave him a cheeky smile.

'That would be an honour, madame,' said Joachim, with a big grin that showed his bright teeth.

Molly grinned back, and, now totally understanding why the other women had been a little unsteady on their feet, made her way out of the annexe and back to the main party.

She saw Charlotte again, over by the drinks, and made her way across to her, smiling at the other pirates, who nodded to her and grinned at her as she went.

'Whew,' she said when she reached her friend. 'That was an experience and a half …'

Charlotte looked at Molly in concern. 'He didn't … hurt you, did he?'

'Hurt me?' Molly laughed. 'No, not at all. But I tell you what … that man can share my bed any night!'

'Molly!' scolded Charlotte. 'How can you say such a thing?'

Molly looked slyly at Charlotte. 'Oh come on, Charlotte. Don't tell me you've never wondered what it might be like to be fucked by … by such a man?'

'No, I have not,' said Charlotte. But the way her eyes strayed to the windows, which now sported two more women who were busy having the ride of their lives, told Molly another story.

'Never mind,' said Molly. 'So who was that chap I saw you talking to then? Is he a pirate prince?'

As they chatted away, the party continued around them, and Charlotte was distant. She was wondering what was happening to them, whether or not they would ever be freed, and whether or not she, like Molly, would end up succumbing to the lure of the men who seemed to be there for the taking.

13

The girl cried out again and her chest flushed bright red as the orgasm overtook her.

Her hands clenched on the bedcovers and she moaned and squirmed as James worked his big cock in and out of her pussy.

Captain Mirabella, watching through a hidden peephole, smiled. The boy certainly seemed ready.

As he watched, the girl rose up again to the peak of pleasure, and wailed as she came once more, coating James's cock with glistening fluid. A ring of white, female cum also ringed the base of his member.

James pulled out, his cock cresting impressively in the dim light of the cabin. The girl was panting and babbling to herself, her hands quivering and her stomach trembling as she continued to orgasm.

James smiled, and encouraged the girl onto her hands and knees. Once she was in position, he gently inserted his cock into her pussy from behind, and pushed forward. The girl gargled deep in her throat and clutched at the sheets.

'Oh no, no, no … ' she babbled. 'Not again. Not more …'

'Ssshhhhh,' said James, and slowly started to fuck her

deeply. His movements pushing her up the bed.

'Oh. My. G – God!' the girl cried. 'Oh. Yes. Fuck. Yes. Fuck me with that amazing cock!'

And James obeyed. He started to fuck her harder, deeper, and faster.

Mirabella felt her own pussy juicing up as she watched. The girl was certainly enjoying the experience. Beside her stood Lucy, watching Mirabella's reaction while listening to the litany of pleasure coming from the other room.

Mirabella flicked a look at Lucy.

'My dear,' she said. 'If you would be so kind …' She gestured to her tight velvet pants, and Lucy grinned and dropped to her knees.

The girl in the next room was now howling with pleasure as she came over and over on the cock that was thrusting into her.

She screamed as a particularly powerful orgasm took her body, and slumped on the bed momentarily, her eyes flickering closed as the pleasure caused her brain to shut down.

Mirabella felt cool, gentle fingers slide her pants down over her shapely bottom, followed by a hot, warm, wet mouth, as Lucy went to work on her, sucking and licking her gently, and running her pierced tongue over and around her sensitive clitoris.

James was unrelenting in the other room. He continued to pleasure the poor girl, sending her up and down in orgasmic pain. She cried out, came again and again, and when she thought it might be over, then James changed his position slightly, making his cock slide wetly against her clitoris, and sending her over the top once more.

Mirabella shuddered as Lucy's clever lips and tongue

suckled her gently to her own orgasm. She moaned deep in her chest as she felt her pussy flood with liquid, to be licked and swallowed by the eager Lucy.

Her breathing returned to normal, and she felt Lucy pull up her leggings once more and return to her side. She smiled at Mirabella coyly.

'I hope the Captain is pleased,' she said.

'I am very pleased,' said Mirabella. 'You have done a near perfect job with the boy.'

Lucy's face creased in a slight frown.

Mirabella grinned. '… And with my own pleasure, of course.'

She looked again through the peephole to see that James was now fucking the poor girl's ass. She was totally out of it, collapsed on the bed, but James was still going strong. The boy had incredible stamina and staying power.

'Should I show you the final proof?' asked Lucy.

Mirabella nodded. She needed to see that the conditioning and training of the boy had been successful.

Lucy dipped in a small curtsey and hurried off.

After a moment, Mirabella heard a gentle knock on the door of the bedroom. She looked intently into the room.

James raised his head. 'Yes?'

Lucy's voice. 'James? It's me, Lucy.'

James smiled. He liked Lucy. He liked fucking her and he liked what she did for him.

'Come in.'

The door opened, and Lucy entered, smiling at James.

She took in the sight of the other girl, face down on the bed, James's large cock buried in her ass, and her hands clenching and scrabbling at the bed sheets as she continued to cum, even as James plundered her depths.

Lucy moved over to where James was standing. Her hands stroked his bare chest and ran up to his neck. She raised her head and kissed him gently on the lips.

'How's it going?' she asked.

'Good,' said James. 'I love how the girls respond.'

Lucy nodded, and flicked a look over to where she knew Mirabella was watching.

'Time for your own relief, I think,' she murmured.

James grinned. 'I thought you'd never offer.'

Without missing a stroke, James let Lucy move closer to him, and as he continued to fuck deeply the poor girl on the bed, Lucy licked her lips, and pressed them gently to James's chest. She kissed him, and then moved across to his left nipple. As her lips found it, so James moaned and stiffened, his thrusting movements becoming more ragged.

Lucy teased his nipple with her teeth, stroking his sides and back with her hands.

Suddenly, James cried out, and his thrusting slowed. The girl on the bed felt her bowels filled with his hot cum as he poured himself into her. She cried out a final time, and spasmed on his cock, helping to milk his cum from him.

Lucy cooed and stroked James, kissing and licking his nipple in appreciation.

When he had finished cumming, Lucy extricated herself from him. His dick slipped from the girl's ass with a plop, and white, creamy cum leaked from her asshole and down her leg. She was utterly exhausted and spent. James had been fucking her for around two hours, and she had orgasmed so many times that she had lost count.

But it wasn't until Lucy had stimulated his nipples that James himself had been able to cum.

Mirabella nodded to herself. Perfect. The boy was a super-stud, able to go for hours, and to pleasure any woman who would pay for him. But in order for him to find release, only Lucy, Mirabella and James himself knew the trick.

Now they could see about Captain Bloodstock and his competition … Just wait until he clapped eyes on James!

14

Charlotte lay in her bed looking at the ceiling. In the next room, she could hear Molly. And Molly was, as usual, enjoying the attentions of Joachim.

Charlotte closed her eyes and tried to imagine what was happening. She had heard Joachim arrive about five minutes ago, then there had been various rustlings and scrapings against the wall. Now she could imagine that they were in bed together. Kissing. Stroking.

She could clearly hear Joachim moaning gently to himself, no doubt as Molly ran her hand over his cock. Charlotte wondered what it might be like to hold such a man in her own hand. To feel the weight of his cock, to touch the veins and sense the heat coming from it.

There was a loud exhale of male breath from the next room, followed by gentle slurping sounds. Charlotte imagined that Molly was on her hands and knees, the large cockhead between her lips, gently sucking at it, massaging it with her hands, but unable to get very much of it at all into her small mouth, no matter how hard she tried.

Joachim's moans became more strident, and Charlotte wondered if she might be able to get his cock into her own mouth. She felt a small tingle in her pussy. A slight *clench* as though her body was telling her that she should be looking to try this soon.

The sounds of sucking and moaning stopped. Then there was creaking, and Molly giggled. Charlotte imagined that they had changed position, and that now Molly was lying under Joachim, his hands positioned either side of her head, and his big, 12-inch dick swaying just by Molly's shaven pussy.

She closed her eyes again, and her hand drifted down to her own pussy, currently sporting a fine down of hair. She rubbed it gently, and enjoyed the feeling of her fingers against the skin of her pussy lips.

She heard Molly moan in pleasure, and knew that Joachim was slowly allowing his cock to enter her, stretching the walls of her pussy aside as he penetrated her deeper and deeper. Charlotte allowed her own fingers to stray deeper in her own folds, gently stroking her clit and sending small waves of pleasure through her body.

'Oh my God, you're so deep!'

Charlotte clearly heard Molly's whisper through the wall. Her words were followed by a loud moan of pleasure, and a gentle, rhythmic tapping on the wall.

Charlotte imagined the scene, as her own hand rubbed against her clit. Molly was on her back, this big black man was positioned over her, his large cock buried deep in her pussy, and as Molly moaned, he was slowly thrusting in and out of her body.

She imagined seeing his cock coated with her juices, gleaming as it emerged, and then plunging swiftly back into her, lubricated by her moisture.

The tapping grew louder and faster, and Molly cried out in pleasure, moaning as the first of many orgasms was wrenched from her body by her skilful lover.

Charlotte rubbed faster too, trying to keep in rhythm with what was being done to her friend, and all the time trying to imagine what it might feel like to have Joachim fuck her like that too.

The rhythmic rapping grew quicker, and faster. So fast now that Charlotte couldn't believe that someone could actually fuck at that speed. And then it suddenly stopped, and at the same time, Molly screamed, 'I'm cummmmminnnnnnggggg!' and descended into an incomprehensible babble of laughter and crying and moaning as she came fast and hard on that big black cock.

Charlotte rubbed her clit faster, bringing herself to a small orgasm that had her eyes tight shut and small sparks of electricity arcing through her body. She breathed faster as she came, a small squeak of pleasure escaping from her lips.

As she descended from her plateau, she heard more rustling and movement from next door. Then she heard the door open and close. Joachim was leaving.

Moments later there was a knock on her own door. Charlotte jumped in surprise and moved her fingers away from her pussy, where they had been idly circling, bringing small shocks of pleasure as she descended from her orgasm.

'Who – who is it?' she called.

'Molly. Can I come in?'

'Sure.'

The door opened and Molly came in. Her hair was dishevelled, and she had a red flush over her breastbone and cheeks, evidence of the massive orgasm she had just enjoyed.

'How are you?' asked Molly. 'I've been worried.' She

narrowed her eyes as she took in Charlotte lying on her bunk, her hair as messy as Molly's own, and with a similar tell-tale red flush to her cheeks. 'Have you been …? Did you …?'

Charlotte didn't know where to look. She smiled and looked away.

Molly laughed. 'Sweet little Charlotte … having some fun at last.'

'Well, it's quite tricky, you know. I can hear everything from next door.'

Molly grinned. 'We know. That's why we moved the bed to the other side of this wall. That's why we make so much noise.'

'You did what?'

'Of course!' said Molly proudly. 'After all, if I'm going to have the fuck of my life, I want my best friend to know about it!'

'You are totally incorrigible,' said Charlotte.

'I know,' giggled Molly. 'And you know you should try it.'

'I … I just couldn't,' said Charlotte. 'Just. No.'

'Oh well,' shrugged Molly. 'Your loss. You'll just have to keep listening to me – and I *will* make sure you can hear me – as Joachim and I make love.' Molly stood and pirouetted in the centre of the room. 'There's another party tonight, you know. I can't wait!'

And with that, she swept from Charlotte's room, presumably to get ready.

Charlotte stayed where she was. She quite enjoyed the parties, but really didn't feel safe enough to let any of the men touch her. She sighed. Maybe she should. If Molly was having so much fun, why shouldn't she too? She had nothing to lose, after all, and she was pretty certain that these pirates would never let them go anyway. She might as well have some fun and make herself useful in some way … The alternative was that they might decide she was taking up space and food that could be better used elsewhere, and dump her overboard somewhere.

With this thought, Charlotte got up from her bunk and looked through the dresses that had been left for her in a wardrobe to one side. At least she could look nice, she thought. This might be the last party she got to attend.

15

The sea was still, and the *Nancy*, Captain Bloodstock's ship, was moored just off the coast. As usual there was a party under way on board. Pirate ladies and gentlemen paraded on the deck, while in the extensive cabins below, there was much in the way of liaisons, dangerous and otherwise.

The main ballroom was full of folk in their finest attire, all sipping wines and spirits from far off lands – or rather, that was where they had originated. They had actually all been plundered from the many ships that crossed the seas; all booty for the pirates.

With everyone on board the *Nancy* gearing up for a night of debauchery and drink, no-one noticed a second ship approaching around the rocks. Its black shape hugged the land, and had anyone been watching, they would have noticed that there was no flag flying.

Slowly, the second ship approached the *Nancy* …

Captain Mirabella was checking that all was ready before she made her final approach and attack on the *Nancy*. She had all her best men lined up on deck, and at the end of the line stood James. He was a little nervous, but the weeks and weeks of confinement, sexual experimentation and various brainwashing techniques had moulded him into exactly what Mirabella wanted: a hard working, hard fucking, pirate lad. He was totally devoted to her and would do anything for her.

Mirabella's mind drifted back to the previous night, when she had summoned James to her own cabin … and he had proceeded to fuck her into six degrees of heaven before she had finally allowed him to cum deep in her mouth. She smiled at the thought.

Mirabella looked over her men, each of them armed with a cutlass and a pistol, each dressed in tight leathers and chain, and each with a mission in the forthcoming attack.

Mirabella wanted no-one actually killed … well … not unless it was to protect her own crew's life. Instead, she wanted that cowardly Bloodstock and some of his women captured and brought to her to help bolster her own crew.

Bloodstock she wanted for herself – he was a magnificent lover – but the others could choose for themselves … and who knew, maybe they would find partners who could match them?

She readied the men, and gave James an appraising look. He seemed perfect for the part, and this was his first raid, so hopefully he would perform well.

As Mirabella's ship, the *Velvet Pearl*, drew closer to the *Nancy*, so Mirabella and her men tensed. Not long now …

Molly's eyes rolled back in her head as Joachim continued to pump his rock-hard dick into her pussy from behind. She was in the pleasure annexe once more, breasts leaning on the window frame and looking out into the main ballroom as Joachim expertly fucked her.

The pleasure was intense, and Molly felt her insides clenching, trying to grip hold of the invader that was giving her so much excitement. She could feel every inch of Joachim's 12-inch shaft as he pounded it into her over and over again, bringing her to shuddering orgasm.

Outside the pleasure room, as usual, was Charlotte. She was standing in the corner, again her usual spot, watching everything that was happening. Her own pussy was throbbing and tingling, and very damp, as she watched her friend being fucked. Molly's cries and moans of pleasure, plus the way her hands gripped the window ledge and her eyes rolled back in her head, showed Charlotte that she was enjoying this immensely.

Charlotte again wondered why she could not herself take a man, why she was so hesitant at taking the ultimate step. She really didn't know, except that she just didn't feel brave enough.

There was a slight judder to the deck, as though the ship had nudged up against something, and the assembled pirates staggered slightly, drinks sloshing over the sides of filled glasses. There was a murmur as people started to discuss what the jolt might have been.

Charlotte's eyes drifted around the room, and came to rest on the figure of a man standing by one of the doors. She narrowed her eyes. He seemed familiar.

The man made his way into the room, as though looking for something. Charlotte watched him as he moved. He was very graceful, and the material of his breeches hugged his muscular thighs nicely … Charlotte shook her head and admonished herself. See what happens? All you can think about these days …

Then, the man's face clicked with her. It was the lad from the *Providence,* she was sure of it. She couldn't remember his name, but he had been working there with Molly.

Charlotte kept her eyes on the man, and started to make her own way around the room toward the annexe, where Molly was currently howling out another massive orgasm as Joachim evidently did something to her with his mouth. She stopped by the window.

'Molly!' she hissed to her friend. 'Molly!'

Molly was breathing hard, but opened her eyes and looked lazily at Charlotte. 'Oh. Hi, Charlotte. I'm … I'm … *oh God* … How are you …? *Yes* … Happy?'

Charlotte frowned. 'Molly, stop that for a moment, will you? Look over there. Isn't that the lad from the *Providence?*'

Molly closed her eyes in pleasure and moaned deep in her throat. 'Shit, he's good, Charlotte. He's so, so, good … *ahhh ahhh ahhh oooohhhhh.*'

Charlotte shook her friend by the arm. 'Molly!' She was getting cross now. 'There's time for that later. Now look …'

Molly opened her eyes and gave Charlotte a look. 'Okay. Hold your petticoats. Which man?'

She looked out at the crowd, and spotted James, who was standing now by the back window, keeping an eye on the assembled crowd.

'Oh yes, he's … *Oh, fuck, Joachim, that's good … mmm* … Yes, he looks like James from the boat.'

'James. Was that his name?' Charlotte asked.

'Yes … yes, James. I'm sure of it,' said Molly as she closed her eyes and tensed her hands once more. '*Oh God, oh yes, I'm … I'm … I'm cumming again!*'

She was breathing heavily as her body rocked in

orgasm once more. As she recovered, she looked at Charlotte.

'You know you really ought to try some of this. It's exquisite ...'

Charlotte huffed, and moved away into the room. She wasn't sure if James would recognise either her or Molly. He had known Molly longer, of course, but their months in captivity had changed their look somewhat. Their hair was loose and unbraided (and Molly's was somewhat dishevelled at the moment) and of course they were wearing party dresses – pirate style.

Charlotte noticed by the doors some other men; men she'd not seen before. Maybe they were newcomers to the party?

At that moment, all the new faces drew their cutlasses and let out a roar. Charlotte squeaked in fright and tried to make herself invisible by the wall. James, his own cutlass drawn, stepped with the other men through the room, herding the partying people to one end. The music had stopped as the small group of musicians had also been moved along with the rest, and there was a restless, worried mumbling coming from the crowd.

In the pleasure annexe, Molly's head had ducked back, but there was no hiding in there, as one of the new pirates went in, and emerged moments later with Joachim and another large black man, both hurriedly adjusting their lower clothing, and Molly, who looked very small indeed beside them.

It was then that James noticed Molly. He strode over to her, and looked her straight in the eyes.

'Molly?' he asked, not quite believing his eyes.

'James,' said Molly.

'But ... what ... what are you doing here? I thought you'd been lost ... That's amazing!'

'Charlotte is here too,' said Molly, her eyes flickering over to where Charlotte was standing.

James looked over at her, his eyes widening in recognition. 'Charlotte?'

Charlotte looked at the floor. She had no idea what was happening, and really didn't want to be a part of it.

James looked around, realising that some of Mirabella's other men were looking at him.

'Follow my lead,' he hissed at Molly. Then, to the rest of the room he shouted, 'Good evening to all of you fine people. I expect you're wondering what's happening … Well, it's just a little pillage … Something to keep you on your toes.'

A murmur ran around the room as another figure pushed open the main door with a bang. It was Captain Mirabella. Her hair was pinned up on her head, her make-up was perfect, she wore a frilled blouse under a leather jerkin, her breasts pressing tightly against the material, and her legs were clad in a pair of midnight blue velvet leggings that hugged her legs and ass perfectly. Setting off her legs were a pair of thigh-high boots of black leather, polished to a gleaming shine.

'Yo, ho, ho,' she said with a smile. 'And what pickings have we here?'

She looked at James, who grinned back at her. 'We have some lovely wenches …' he said, grabbing Molly's arm and pulling her out of the crowd. He left her standing in front of Mirabella and headed back into the throng to grab Charlotte. Both girls stood there sadly, not quite knowing what they should do, but Molly caught James winking at her, so she at least felt that things might work out okay.

'Lovely,' said Mirabella. 'And of the men?'

Molly nudged James. 'If we're being taken

somewhere else, can I have Joachim come with us?' she whispered.

James nodded. 'There are some,' he said. 'This one …'

James stepped over to where the two black men were standing. He grabbed one by the arm, and shot a look at Molly. She shook her head briefly, nodding to the other.

'This one … is no good,' James finished. 'We'll take the other!' And with that he grabbed Joachim's arm and led him to stand with the girls.

'Is that all?' asked Mirabella.

'It's all we need to make our point,' said James.

Mirabella nodded. It was a point well made.

'Come,' she ordered, then turned on a pointed heel and strode from the room.

James pushed the three in front of him. Joachim was initially reluctant, but Molly grabbed his hand and told him that it would be okay. Trust her.

Charlotte also realised that all was not quite what it seemed here. Maybe this was her rescue? She followed Molly and Joachim without a word, hoping that, in this case, they were heading out of the frying pan and into something somewhat better.

As they emerged onto the deck, another group of pirates arrived, carrying a figure with a potato sack on his head.

'Is this Bloodstock?' asked Mirabella.

'Sure is,' said one of the pirates. 'Struggles a lot!'

Mirabella smiled and pulled off the sack to reveal Captain Bloodstock's reddened face.

'What? What is the meaning of this?' Cradle blustered. 'You can't do this!'

'Ah. But we can. And have,' said Mirabella. 'Now you're coming with us.'

The small boarding party then made their way along

the deck to a gap in the railings where some boards had been laid across, connecting the *Nancy* with the *Velvet Pearl*. They headed across the planks, and when they were all safely on the other side, some of Mirabella's men removed the planks, and the *Velvet Pearl* started to move away from the *Nancy*.

As they drifted away, they heard, in the distance, the party music start up again … as though nothing had happened.

16

Captain Mirabella lounged on her bed in her cabin. It had been a good evening. She had managed to second-guess Captain Bloodstock and put both him and some of his own 'guests' under her control.

But she was not a bad pirate – at least, not in that sense. She wouldn't hurt the newcomers. On the contrary, she hoped they would find life on board the *Velvet Pearl* quite pleasurable.

There was a rap on the door.

'Come,' she said.

The door opened to reveal Cradle, with Lucy standing at his side, her hand poised on her cutlass, just in case of any problems.

Cradle stepped into the room. 'Captain Mirabella,' he said. 'Thank you so much for your invitation …'

Mirabella smiled. 'It's all my pleasure, Captain. Or it will be … Thank you, Lucy, that will be all.'

Lucy nodded and left the room, closing the door behind her.

'I thought we had an agreement,' said Cradle, moving over to where Mirabella kept her liquor. 'But you seem to have broken it.'

'Oh, Captain,' said Mirabella, sliding her legs off the bed and moving across to him. 'You *know* we are pirates. And pirates don't keep agreements. All's fair in love and war.'

She took the poured glass of bourbon from him and sipped it. 'Help yourself,' she said.

Cradle poured himself another glass. 'So, what's the deal? How does this pan out?'

Mirabella placed her glass down on a table and moved back to Cradle, running her fingers up his chest and over his shoulders, cupping the back of his head in her hands.

'I think I should show you,' she said.

She went to a closet, looked back at Cradle, and made a 'come here' signal with her index finger.

She pushed at the closet door, and it swung inward to reveal a hidden passage from her room. Cradle shook his head and followed her down the passage.

Every so often there was a small slit cut into the wall, and Cradle realised that these allowed Mirabella to see into all the cabins on this deck.

They came to a halt beside one of the slits. Mirabella peered in, and then gestured for Cradle to look as well.

In the room beyond, Cradle could see the girl Molly. She was wearing just a white nightshift, and as he watched, she pulled it up and over her head, revealing her naked body. Her breasts were full, and jiggled nicely as she moved, and her pubic hair was absent, having been freshly shaven. Her hips curved in, giving her a nice waist, and her long hair fell down around her shoulders.

She shifted position slightly, and Cradle saw that the slave Joachim was there also. He was standing next to the bed, and Cradle almost gasped when he saw the size of his cock. It stood out from his body and was large, long and thick.

Mirabella licked her lips in anticipation. She loved watching her crew entertain themselves. It gave her a certain *frisson*.

Molly sank to her knees in front of Joachim and gently took his large cock in her hands. She rubbed it up and down, dribbling a little saliva onto it to provide lubrication and then putting her lips to the bell end, letting her tongue lick lazily around the head before allowing it to enter her mouth.

As she suckled on it, Cradle noted that she really had to stretch to open her mouth. The man's cock just would not fit. But soon she was sucking and gagging on the shaft as she worked it up and down with her hands and mouth. Kissing it and stroking it, and also running her hands down to Joachim's balls and fondling them gently as she continued to service his massive manhood.

Joachim encouraged her to stand, and he wrapped his large hands around her small body, kissing her tenderly on the lips and stroking her pale skin. Molly moaned in pleasure, and Cradle realised that she had developed great feelings for this slave. In her hands he was a pussycat, willing and eager to please.

The couple fell onto the bed, still kissing and touching each other. Joachim picked Molly up and placed her on her hands and knees – a position she knew well, and which gave her the most intense orgasms.

Mirabella gave a small gasp of pleasure herself as she watched the massive black cock disappear into Molly's tiny white pussy. Molly gasped too, only a lot louder, and soon she was panting and gasping as Joachim thrust powerfully into her, over and over again.

'She seems to be enjoying herself,' whispered Cradle.

As Molly screamed with pleasure, Mirabella nodded, and gestured for Cradle to follow her. They moved further along the passage, Molly's cries and exhortations of *More!* and *Harder!* fading into the distance.

They stopped at another slit in the wall and peered through. This time Cradle saw James standing in the room. He had a glass of wine in his hand, and he gave it to Charlotte.

Charlotte took it from him. 'Thank you.'

James smiled at her. 'Seems that we didn't really get the chance to become properly acquainted before.'

'Indeed,' said Charlotte with a smile. She sipped the wine. It was white and cold.

She looked up at James. He was very handsome indeed, and seemed to have a certain confidence he had been lacking before.

He poured himself a glass of wine too, and sat down on the bed next to Charlotte.

'Cheers.'

They clinked glasses together, and drank.

'I think,' said James after a moment, 'that if I had known you under different circumstances, then we could have been good friends.'

Charlotte blushed. 'I think,' she said, 'that you might be right.'

All of her confused feelings and emotions were coming to the fore now, and she realised that she couldn't just drift along on Molly's coattails. She had to make some decisions, as otherwise she was going to end up like the slatterns who mopped the bilge from the decks, or who cleaned out the head. Wasted and broken people, with no real lives and nothing to strive for. That wasn't for her.

She sipped her wine again, and let her hand rest on James's leg for a moment. She looked into his eyes. 'I think, indeed, that we could have been *very* good friends.'

James grinned at her, and Charlotte realised that when he smiled, the whole room lit up around them. He stood and placed his wine on the table, and then remained standing with his back to her.

Charlotte was momentarily confused – but that was the old her … She needed to be decisive, so she stood and went to James, placing her hands on his shoulders. He turned, his own hands on her waist, and now they were face to face.

Charlotte looked into his eyes, and he looked down at her. And then, after a moment, they kissed.

For Charlotte, it was as though she had gone to heaven. His lips were so soft, and the kiss so deep and loving. She had thought about that sort of kiss for so long, and here she was …

James was very taken with Charlotte too. She was pretty, intelligent, and, it turned out, a darn good kisser.

Having made her mind up, Charlotte ran her hands down James's chest and started to unbutton his shirt. He made no move to stop her, and so she soon had him naked to the waist. She kissed his neck, and started to trail small kisses down his chest.

It was when she reached his nipples that he stiffened, his cock growing another inch – and it had been straining as it was. Charlotte had unwittingly stumbled across his secret.

James smiled to himself. Time for some fun!

Charlotte squealed with delight as James took her in his arms and tumbled her onto the bed. She struggled to get her dress and undergarments off, but soon she and

James were naked, and she was lying under him on the bed, arms above her head, wondering what the old Charlotte had been so worried about.

James smiled at her, and gently massaged and spread her sex with his fingers. She was soaking wet. Charlotte moaned gently, enjoying the sensation of someone else playing with her. She moved her hand and found his cock. And her eyes opened wide. He was bigger than she had expected.

She cast a glance downwards, and took in his impressive manhood, thick, long and with a nice head that bulged from the stalk. She stroked her hand over it momentarily.

In for a penny, she thought, and pulled him gently to her entrance. Then she held her breath as he positioned himself, before thrusting slowly into her.

The feeling as the large cock stretched the walls of her pussy apart was indescribable. After a moment, she felt him pull back, leaving her empty momentarily, before the lovely cock was back again, filling her up once more.

She spread her legs as wide as she could to give James access, and lay back and let him start to make love to her in the way that she had always imagined. Her breath fluttering in gasps as the pleasure suffused her body, and her hands moving to clutch and hold James's hot body to her as she finally felt an orgasm pull slowly from her pussy, expanding along her legs and up her body, igniting all her nerve endings in an explosion of light and electricity.

'That was intense,' said Mirabella from the hidden corridor.

Cradle swallowed. It had been most intense. Watching the couples enjoy themselves had roused his own ardour, and he was wondering what Mirabella had in mind …

'Maybe we should retire to your cabin?' he suggested. 'To … to discuss things further.'

Mirabella smiled at him. He had always been her favourite pirate. 'Of course,' she said. 'Lead the way.'

As the sun sank below the horizon, the crew of the *Velvet Pearl* enjoyed their evening. The ship rocked gently from side to side as the couples within took their pleasure; and if you listened very closely, you could hear the sounds – male and female – of contentment. Cries of the affirmative, and to various deities. Demands not to stop, and to go deeper and harder and faster and slower …

Life as a pirate certainly had its benefits.

About the Author

Athena Michaels lives in London with her husband John and their two cats Ben and Jerry.

Romance and Erotica From Telos

SINFUL PLEASURES

<u>ATHENA MICHAELS</u>
AWAKENING JESSICA

<u>ROBERTA STEELE</u>
BYTE ME!

ROMANTIC ENCOUNTERS

<u>CATHERINE SERIES BY JULIETTE BENZONI</u>
1: CATHERINE: ONE LOVE IS ENOUGH
2: CATHERINE
3: BELLE CATHERINE (coming soon)
4: CATHERINE: HER GREAT JOURNEY (coming soon)
5: CATHERINE: A TIME FOR LOVE (coming soon)
6: A TRAP FOR CATHERINE (coming soon)
7: CATHERINE: THE LADY OF MONTSALVY (coming soon)

<u>HELEN MCCABE</u>
A GARDEN FAIR
HIGHWAY TO FEAR
HOSTAGE TO LOVE
IN SEARCH OF LOVE
LOVE IN HIDING
THE HOUSE ON THE MOUNTAIN
THE PRICE OF LOVE
WHEN LOVE RIDES OUT

www.ingramcontent.com/pod-product-compliance
Lightning Source LLC
Chambersburg PA
CBHW060803210726